812.8

ONE NIGHT TO
WEDDING VOWS

ONE NIGHT TO WEDDING VOWS

BY

KIM LAWRENCE

First published in Great Britain 2016
By Mills & Boon, an imprint of HarperCollins*Publishers*
1 London Bridge Street, London, SE1 9GF

Large Print edition 2016

© 2016 Kim Lawrence

ISBN: 978-0-263-26220-9

Our policy is to use papers that are natural, renewable and recyclable products and made from wood grown in sustainable forests. The logging and manufacturing processes conform to the legal environmental regulations of the country of origin.

Printed and bound in Great Britain
by CPI Antony Rowe, Chippenham, Wiltshire

CHAPTER ONE

THE PLACE DIDN'T fall silent as Sergio Di Vittorio walked through the casino but there was a discernible hush in the room, an air of expectancy as the elderly aristocrat walked in ahead of two tall, dark, suited figures. The heavier set of the two stayed by the entrance while the other followed his employer, remaining a respectful pace behind the older man as he continued his regal progress.

From where he was standing, one shoulder propped against a marble pillar, Raoul's sensually designed lips curved in a cynical smile from which affection was not totally absent as he watched his grandfather's stately arrival. In the periphery of his vision he remained aware of the middle-aged guy, eyes glazed with febrile excitement, who continued to throw good money after bad on the roulette wheel. It had been like watching a car crash, now only a matter of how many innocent victims he'd take with him...a wife, a kid...?

The reckless gleam in Raoul's own deep-set dark eyes owed more to the brandy in his hand than the spin of a wheel. Each to his own drug of choice, Raoul thought, with a lazy tolerance. He turned, a faint ironic smile of self-mockery curving his lips as he found himself automatically straightening his spine as his grandfather got closer. *Old habits die hard*, he thought to himself, and his grandfather had strong views on good posture.

The autocratic head of the diverse family businesses and guardian of the family name had strong views on most things. Gambling, for one. Not really surprising considering his only son, Raoul and Jamie's father, had blown his brains out when the full extent of his gambling debts became public.

Sergio could have hushed up the scandal and covered his son's debts—the amount involved was small change to him—but instead he had chosen to tell his son to stand on his own two feet and be a man.

Did he regret it?

Did he blame himself?

Raoul doubted it. Sergio's self-belief did not allow for doubts. Raoul's youthful anger had been reserved for the father who had taken the easy way out and left them. It was hard for a kid to comprehend that level of self-destructive desperation, or to get his head around the fact that addicts were inherently selfish. Even the years of adult understanding did not take away the bitterness or the memories of a lonely child, but Jamie had always been there for him, the older brother who had fought his battles until Raoul had got big and tough enough to hold his own.

The long fingers of the hand Raoul dug into the pocket of his tailored dark trousers flexed as his mind drifted back. He could almost feel his brother's warm fingers tightening around his own as their grandfather broke the news. The moment was etched in his memory: the single tear rolling, in what had seemed like slow motion, down his older brother's face; the metronomic tick of a clock on the wall; his grandfather's deep voice explaining that they would be living with him now.

Confusion and fear had clutched at his stomach, the heavy ache of a sob in his throat held there by the desperate need to please his grandfather. He'd saved his tears for the privacy of his pillow.

Raoul pulled his drifting thoughts back to the present, his mouth a hard line as his heavy-lidded, cynical stare drifted to the glass he lifted in a silent salute: *absent friends!* As the years went on, the pillow had given way to brandy. Or maybe he had simply lost the ability to cry altogether. Maybe he'd lost the ability to feel as normal people did.

Tears would not bring his brother back. Jamie was gone.

He lowered his gaze, his chest lifting as the dark mesh of his lashes shut out the grief. He refused to acknowledge the buffeting of a fresh wave of despair that no amount of brandy could numb.

'You were missed at the wake.' Sergio tilted his head to the spinning roulette wheel. 'So, you have decided to follow in your father's footsteps?'

With a jerk Raoul's head came up. 'It is always an option, I suppose,' he drawled. 'And you know what they say…an addictive personality is hereditary.'

Sergio responded to the remark with one of his inimitable shrugs. 'I considered the possibility.'

The frank admission wrenched a hard, cracked laugh from Raoul's throat. 'Of course you did.'

'No, you both escaped the taint but you are an adrenaline junkie, just like Ja—' The old man stopped and swallowed hard several times before continuing. 'Your brother always said that— He… Jam…'

Unable to watch his grandfather struggle for control, Raoul cut across him, throwing out harshly, 'That if I didn't kill myself climbing it would be behind the wheel of one of my cars.'

For a moment his brother's voice sounded so real that he almost turned expecting to see the familiar smiling face—*you're an adrenaline junkie, little brother, and one of these days you'll kill yourself...* The irony was like a punch to the gut.

But Jamie had been the one to die young, not because he had taken a corner too fast but because life was just not fair.

Raoul took a deep swallow of the brandy swirling in his glass as anger circled in his head. It took a few jaw-clenching seconds before he trusted his voice to continue.

'I never expected to see you slumming it in a place like this, but I have to admit you do know how to make an entrance.' It was true. Even in his eighties Sergio Di Vittorio made an imposing figure, dressed as always in black, the abundant silver-streaked, collar-length hair catching the light cast by the glittering chandeliers overhead.

If his emotions hadn't flatlined he might be curious about why his grandfather was here but Raoul continued to feel nothing. He took a swallow of brandy and checked—yes, nothing.

This lying to himself was actually something he might be quite good at.

'People were asking after you.'

Raoul tipped his head down. Sergio was a tall man, six feet, deep chested and broad of shoulder, but Raoul had been four inches taller than his grandfather since he was fifteen. It still felt somehow not quite right, almost disrespectful, to look down on him.

'Good party, was it?' He slumped back against the column, the lazy posture giving him less height advantage. He raised his glass to his lips, the gesture going some way to hiding his expression as he thought, *When did you get so damned old?*

There was nothing like a funeral to make a person aware of their own mortality and that of those they loved…precious few of whom were left.

He pushed away the dark thought and took another slug of the brandy. It slid down his throat, settling in his stomach with a warmth that did nothing to alleviate the coldness that permeated his entire body, a *coldness* that had nothing to do with the temperature in the room.

Sergio impatiently waved away a suited figure who started to approach, and his bodyguard made sure no more attempts were made.

'We need to talk.'

Raoul had never reacted well to orders. But this was his grandfather so he ignored how the command chafed, allowing his attention to be drawn by the cry of the middle-aged guy at the roulette wheel. It was hard to tell if it was jubilance or misery, but the distraction had served its purpose.

'Raoul...!'

Raoul gave himself a mental shake and turned back to his grandfather. 'We *are* talking.'

Sergio's lips thinned in predictable annoyance. 'In private.' He made a sharp stabbing gesture with his leonine head indicating that Raoul should follow and walked off.

After a pause Raoul levered himself off the cold surface, flexed his shoulder blades, and did so.

Once the door of the panelled, private room was closed Sergio wasted no time.

'Your brother is dead.'

Any number of bitter, sarcastic responses occurred to Raoul but he clamped his lips tight on them. He had been the one who had discovered his brother's lifeless body on the floor of his kitchen and the image still wouldn't let go. An aneurysm the post mortem said. It seemed his brother had been walking around with a ticking time bomb in his chest for years and he hadn't even known it was there.

'You here to tell me life goes on?' He'd read up on it and discovered that what had killed Jamie wasn't that uncommon. Now he found himself walking down the street looking into faces of strangers and wondering who would be next.

'Not for everyone. I'm dying.'

Raoul, who had walked over to the velvet-draped window, spun back, fighting off the childish desire to cover his ears. After a moment's silence he shrugged and dropped his long, lean length into one of the leather sofas.

'We are all dying.'

Or was it only the people he loved?

He closed his eyes and did a silent body count...

the mother he barely remembered, his father, his brother, his wife… No! She didn't count. He hadn't loved Lucy by the end. In fact, he had loathed her, but she was gone and they all had one thing in common: *him*.

Perhaps I should come with a government health warning?

The black humour of the thought drew a harsh laugh from his stiff lips while in his head the scornful voice retorted, *Perhaps you should stop feeling so bloody sorry for yourself?*

'It's cancer,' his grandfather said, at Raoul's response. 'Inoperable. Their best bet is that I have six months.' The older man delivered the information without emotion. 'Though I've never trusted quacks.'

Raoul surged to his feet, denial in every muscle of his taut, powerful body. 'That isn't possible.' Their eyes, both pairs dark and shot with silver flecks, connected and after a moment of contact Raoul swallowed.

'Sorry.' His teeth clenched at the laughable inadequacy of the word.

But Sergio simply brushed away the comment with a gesture of his hand. 'Continuity is important to me—you know what I'm talking about.'

Raoul exhaled a long, slow, measured breath and thought, *Hell, not* this, *not* now!

'Your brother was never going to provide an heir.'

Raoul said nothing. This was the closest the older man had ever come to acknowledging his brother's sexuality. He'd never called Jamie's long-term partner, Roberto, anything other than his *friend*. Raoul felt a stab of guilt. He should have stayed for Rob at least—the man had been utterly devastated at the funeral service.

'Jamie is barely cold...' But his skin had been like marble when... Raoul cleared his throat. 'Can't this wait?'

'Time is not a luxury I have.' Sergio saw his grandson wince and took a step forward, adopting the stare that made powerful men sweat, and laid his hands on his grandson's shoulders. 'I made allowances for you after... Lucy died.' Raoul's hooded gaze dropped, a nerve along his jaw clenched. 'But you have to move on.'

'I have moved on.'

A sound of distaste escaped the old man's lips before he turned away. 'I'm not talking about screwing around.'

The uncharacteristic crudeness from his grandfather's lips wiped the last shreds of alcohol-induced haze from Raoul's brain. 'There is no doubt about the diagnosis?'

'None.'

'Sorry,' he said again, knowing that any more tactile or emotional gestures would not be appreciated. His grandfather had a volcanic temperament but he had never encouraged physical displays of emotion in either of his grandsons. It hadn't stopped Jamie, but he… It hadn't come naturally to Raoul. He had learned the advantages of not showing his feelings—his *robot face*, Lucy had called it. Half her twisted pleasure had been seeing her victims suffer.

The older man tipped his head in acknowledgement. 'It will all come to you now. Whether,' he added before the flare of anger in his grandson's dark eyes could spark into flame, 'you want it or not. You will be a powerful man.'

The last man standing.

Whether I want it or not…and I don't!

'That power brings responsibility,' Sergio warned.

It wasn't the time to point out that many considered Raoul a powerful man already. While Jamie had chosen to work for his grandfather, after Harvard Raoul had joined a New York law firm, refused the opportunity to become the youngest partner in the history of that prestigious firm and had instead struck out on his own, ignoring all the voices that said he'd regret it.

No voices now, when just a few years later he had offices in several global capitals with a client list of some of the richest companies and private individuals in the world.

The perfect life, but without the rush of the courtroom he was bored out of his mind! At some point he had stopped being a litigator and become a glorified manager. But his brother was the only person Raoul had confided his frustration to. *Damn you! Why did you have to go?*

'And wealth, of course, but more importantly you will carry on the name. And don't launch into one of your egalitarian rants—'

Raoul cut across him. 'Is this where you say something that begins with, if you want to make a dying old man happy...?'

'Yes.'

'So, moral blackmail.' He spoke without resentment; he could see the logic in his grandfather's approach.

'I may never see my grandchildren.'

He lowered his gaze, though not before Raoul had seen a sheen form in the old man's eyes. But when he looked up again the only thing in those deep-set eyes was a familiar ruthless determination. Raoul dropped the hand he had stretched out and rubbed it along his thigh, his square fingertips white as he pressed into muscle. He sighed.

'But I have time enough to see you married to a woman who will give you children. You can't recapture what you had with Lucy and it's about time you accepted it.'

An image floated into Raoul's head, a laughing face, perfect and beautiful, the way the world had seen his wife... *Recapture...?* Only an insane person would want to recapture the life of undiluted hell he had lived with his blackmailing, toxic wife.

Raoul was not insane!

His marriage had not left him a woman hater. He liked women; women were gorgeous! The problem was *him*. It was a fact painfully proven that when he allowed himself to be emotionally involved with a woman, he simply couldn't trust his own judgement. It was fatally flawed.

So when his grandfather had accused him of screwing around he had not been wrong, nor had it been an accident. Casual sex satisfied a basic need, and if occasionally he was conscious—regardless of how great the sex—of a nebulous *something* missing, it was something that he was willing to live without.

'Anyone in mind?'

His grandfather ignored the sarcastic tone. 'Obviously the choice is yours.'

'Generous of you.'

'This is not a joke. Our family name is not a joke. I do not want to die with a playboy grandson as my sole legacy in life. It's time you faced up to your responsibilities.'

Raoul bit back a retort that hovered over his tongue, hands digging deep in his pockets as he walked towards the ornate marble fireplace. 'So what do you suggest—should I draw up a job spec and work my way through a shortlist of applicants? Or are you, God forbid, suggesting I follow my heart?' The sarcasm spilled over, but Raoul didn't care. The day couldn't get any worse now.

Again his tone fell on infertile ground; instead his grandfather looked thoughtful.

'That is actually not such a bad idea.'

'What, following my heart?' His experience

with Lucy had cured Raoul of any trust in following his heart. The fact that there had been clues with Lucy only rubbed salt in the wound, clues that in any other situation he would not have ignored, but he had been in love and seen only what he had wanted. 'Or advertising?'

The older man flashed him a look. 'Sometimes putting things down in writing focuses the mind. After all, your wife will require certain q...qualities...' Without warning Sergio reached out for support, a sound close to a groan escaping his clamped teeth.

It was all so unexpected that for a moment Raoul froze. Then as the old man staggered the paralysis broke. The resentment of moments earlier evaporated as he sprinted to his grandfather's side, reaching him before he crumpled.

A supportive arm across Sergio's back helped lift him into the nearest chair. Raoul was shocked to feel through the tailored suit, not the solidity and strength that had always been there, but sharp ribs.

This was real. It was happening.

For the first time the reality hit him. His grandfather had been the one constant in his life and now he was dying and nothing Raoul could do would stop it.

The same way he hadn't been able to stop his mother being just another statistic in a flu epidemic, his father shooting out his brains or his brother's big heart bursting. It seemed like a lot of death and loss for one person to take. A curling wave of anger and helplessness washed over him.

He really was the last man standing. He could get drunk and feel sorry for himself or he could… He looked at his grandfather and felt an overwhelming wave of love for the tough, proud old man.

He *could* do something. His grandfather had just told him what he could do, not to stop him dying but to make him die content. He wouldn't have thought twice if it were bone marrow or a kidney he was being asked for, so why hesitate now?

Because losing his right hand would be easy compared to what his grandfather was asking. Marriage had taught him that he could not trust his own judgement when his heart was engaged. And that you could never really know another person, never trust them. So gambling your future and giving up your freedom was insane.

There had to be an alternative and when he sobered up it would be obvious…

'I'll get an ambulance.'

'No…' The hand that covered his was shaking but the voice was stronger now and emphatic as he repeated the prohibition. 'No, no hospitals. It's passed.' The hand that still grasped his grandson's tightened. 'I can't make you do this…today of all days… Jamie would have called me a selfish old—'

'Jamie loved you,' Raoul cut in roughly.

'Your brother loved life.'

Raoul nodded and pretended not to see the tears on the old man's cheeks. 'And you're not saying anything I haven't considered myself.' The expression on his grandfather's grey-tinged face made Raoul glad of the lie.

'You have?'

'I'm not getting any younger.'

'And you want a family?'

Raoul tipped his head, recalling a time when that had been true.

'It is a natural instinct.'

Any instincts he might have possessed had not survived his short marriage to Lucy. Lucy, who'd had a talent and a no-holds-barred policy when it came to inflicting pain in retribution for perceived slights and insults. A year must have passed before, in one of her rages, she had revealed the abortion she had had during the early months of their marriage.

'You think I'd get fat and ugly just to give you a brat!' she'd screamed.

He pushed away the echo in his mind and the image of the lovely face twisted in spite and malice. It was an image he could escape temporarily in the beds of warm, willing women. But it was a good thing that it would never really leave his mind—that way he knew he was never going to risk losing his heart. He visualised that organ safely enclosed in steel; there wasn't a woman alive who could put a dent in his armour.

'Are you sure I can't...?'

'Carlo...' dabbing a hand to the sweat beading his upper lip, Sergio nodded towards the closed door '...knows what to do. You...' Dark eyes sought those of his grandson. 'You know,' he continued huskily, 'what you can do for me. No matter what, you and your brother have given my life a meaning, a richness that it would otherwise have lacked.' The dark eyes clouded as he shook his head. 'I was a bad father.'

Raoul looked into the face of the man who had struggled to show affection, but had always been there for his grandsons. A surge of emotion left an aching occlusion in his throat. A lie was a little thing to pay back the debt he owed this man. He was never going to marry, to fall in love, but what was the harm letting him think…?

'Then I must learn by your mistakes?'

'I'm sure you'll make your own.' A thoughtful expression crossed his heavily lined face. 'Is there anyone?'

Raoul forced a laugh, his dark brows lifting as he responded. 'You will be the first to know and that is a promise.'

'You probably don't want my advice, but I'll give it anyway. Don't make your final selection on looks alone. Obviously no one would expect you to marry someone you didn't find attractive…'

'That's a relief.'

'It may seem cold-blooded but—'

'Shall I take notes?' This conversation would have been one to share with his brother. Jamie would have appreciated it; he and his brother shared the same sense of humour—*had* shared.

The flicker of ironic amusement faded from his eyes.

'Practicality is not a dirty word. You shouldn't leave the important things in life to blind luck. Oh, I know you struck lucky once but you can't rely on that happening again.'

Not on my watch, Raoul thought grimly.

'Marriage should be approached like any other contract.'

Sergio's voice was stronger but his skin was still cast with a worrying greyish tinge. 'I'm sure you're right,' Raoul conceded, then, seeing the suspicious light in his grandparent's eyes, realised he'd agreed too easily. 'Shall I call Carlo now?'

Without waiting for a reply he opened the door and spoke to the man stationed outside.

Before his grandfather had time to relaunch his campaign for a grandchild, a maid who had obviously been waiting in the wings for a nod from the bodyguard appeared carrying a tea tray. Carlo followed her in.

The maid vanished and the big protective figure poured tea, slipping something from a blister pack into his employer's hand before he nodded and left.

'Man of few words.'

The tea seemed to have restored his grand-father, who snorted. 'Coming from you that is amusing, but then your brother was always the talker, I remember—'

Raoul had heard the stories many times be-fore. Some he'd experienced firsthand, but he let his grandfather talk. He seemed to find relating Jamie's exploits cathartic, the boy he had been and the man he had become, a man Sergio had been proud of. Well, in a professional capacity, at least. By the time he got up from his chair—under his own steam—he looked more himself.

On the point of leaving the room Raoul paused and turned back, his expression intense. Bracing himself to lie through his teeth about his readi-ness to marry and procreate, Raoul was surprised and relieved when his grandfather asked his opin-ion on a very different subject.

'I would value your input on something. I was thinking of donating a new wing in your brother's name to the university hospital. Do you think he would have liked that?'

'I think he would have liked that very much, but surely Roberto would be a better person to speak to about it?' His brother's partner was a consultant neurologist at the hospital.

His grandfather looked thoughtful for a moment before nodding. 'He spoke well at the funeral.'

Raoul agreed.

'I might do that. Come walk with me to the car.'

Glad to hear the familiar note of imperious command back in the old man's voice, Raoul followed his grandfather out of the room and through the brightly lit casino.

Out of the air-conditioned cool Raoul barely registered the warmth of the evening but within seconds his grandfather's skin was filmed with moisture. Nevertheless, he rejected the arm Raoul offered with a grunt, moving towards the limo that drew up.

'I'll call tomorrow?'

His grandfather shook his head. 'Next week, as planned. I'm not dying yet.'

Watching the car pull away, Raoul found himself wondering if lying to a dying man could ever be considered the right thing to do.

The question was academic—it was done and he doubted it would be the first lie he told. But how many more would he have to tell, and how far down this road would he need to go to allow his grandfather to die happy?

With an impatient click of his long fingers he started to walk. There was no harm in humouring his grandfather, and Raoul was sure he could string it out until… He didn't want to think about another death today, another loss.

'Dio!' he murmured under his breath as he locked away the memories. To think about the children he might have had, the life he might have led was pointless, that future was lost to him.

He had a new future. Thinking of it stretching out ahead of him, he was conscious of an empty feeling in his chest. He might not have auditioned for the role, but it was his. He *was* the last man standing, or at least the last Di Vittorio standing, which to his grandfather meant the same thing.

CHAPTER TWO

'FINE. I'LL SLEEP with the first man I see!'

It was really hard to maintain any dignity, having just issued a threat worthy of a teenager having a tantrum, thought Lara. Mark's laugh in response only made her madder, so she slammed the door as hard as she could. Lara was slim but she was tall and athletic so the door rattled in its frame.

The first man she saw was the balding middle-aged proprietor of the hotel they had booked into for their *romantic* weekend.

He looked at Lara with concern as she rushed past him into the street, tears coursing down her cheeks.

The blurb had claimed the small hotel was within walking distance of all the main tourist sites, clearly a gross exaggeration. But it hadn't mattered to Lara, who had never had any intention of doing a lot of sightseeing!

How could she have been such a fool?

She had thought Mark was different. *Maybe I'm meant to be alone*, she thought. The prospect wrenched a sob from her throat.

Self-pity, said the voice in her head, *is very un-attractive.* She ignored it and sniffed loudly and angrily.

This would never have happened to Lily, but then no man who took her twin away for a romantic weekend would have acted as though he'd been lured there under false pretences if he discovered she was a virgin.

Was her twin a virgin...?

A thoughtful expression flickered across her face as Lara considered the question. Her twin didn't talk to her much about that sort of thing, but then they hadn't talked about that sort of thing since the boy she'd known Lily had fancied had taken Lara to the Christmas party the year they were sixteen. It was years ago now, and a joke, but Lil hadn't see it that way at the time... What had his name been?

How ironic if Lily was not a virgin, while she, who people assumed had had more lovers than handbags, most definitely was. But then that was people for you—they always assumed the worst.

So Lara had decided a long time ago that life was simpler if you just let them.

People did so love their boxes—Lily was the sensible twin while Lara was the wild child. She liked to party ergo she slept around. Right now she wished she had!

She bit her lip, feeling a fresh rush of tears.

'I hate men, all men and especially Mark Randall!'

For about thirty seconds the outburst made her feel empowered, then like all pointless gestures it left a sense of anticlimax and the knowledge this was her own fault.

It could have been worse—she could have slept with him and *then* discovered he was a pathetic loser. What was it about him that she'd been attracted to in the first place?

Smooth brow pleated, she pondered the question. True, he'd seemed like a considerate boss and he'd noticed her. Everyone noticed her, but Mark had noticed her for her work. He'd said she had potential, and she hadn't minded doing extra work, work way beyond her pay grade, because he appreciated it and he was one of the few men in the building who hadn't tried it on… *Hmm, big clue there, Lara.*

She had decided that there was sensitivity gleaming behind his horn-rimmed spectacles and kindness in his eyes. She'd felt safe around him and love, or the sort *she* wanted, was about feeling safe and secure.

Lara did not want the sort of love that would leave her feeling utterly bereft if she found out her lover or husband was cheating. *Had Dad been a cheat?* Lara didn't know for certain if the charming, charismatic father she had adored had been unfaithful. The clues had all been there, but she had never asked her mum for confirmation. She didn't think she could bear to hear the answer.

Lara never intended to feel *that* way about any man, so while her friends looked for men who made them lose control Lara looked for quite different qualities.

Qualities her new boss had seemed to epitomise. For the first time she was being treated as an equal by someone who saw her as a person and not a sex object, and she had found the combination irresistible.

He was too nice and too professional, she reasoned, to make the first move, which was sweet but a bit frustrating. Not being someone who thought patience or unrequited love were good

things, Lara had set about making him notice
that she could do more than file.

It hadn't been easy and she had even started
to wonder if he was gay, but then right out of the
blue he had asked her: a weekend in Rome. She'd
been waiting for the right man and the right time
and it had finally arrived—or so she'd thought.

True love. It existed, she was sure of it. You
could get sent home from school for wearing your
skirt too short and still be a romantic. You could
party and still want a family and a home.

She was prepared to wait for the right man, but
she saw no reason why the wait had to be boring!
Lara was gregarious and she had always enjoyed
an active social life; men liked her and she enjoyed their company.

She was aware that her lifestyle made many assume that she enjoyed casual sex, but she never
strung men along and if some chose to boast of
a non-existent conquest she lost no sleep over it
or over those who couldn't handle the fact she
wasn't into one-night stands.

The only question had been whether to tell Mark
or not. In the end she'd decided she would—no
relationship should start with secrets. The perfect
opportunity had arisen earlier that night when

he'd been scrolling through his phone and discovered a recent interview with his uncle, the CEO of the firm where they both worked.

'This is what I have to deal with, but no point offending the guy. Look, listen to this…no, this is the part where he rambles on about family values,' he sneered. 'And this is the bit when he says one-night stands are—'

'Mark?' He looked up, seeming to notice for the first time that she was standing there wearing the matching silk bra and pants she had spent so long choosing.

I'm competing with a smartphone.

'Actually, Mark.' Her self-esteem was pretty robust and the fact that he wasn't jumping on her was what made Mark different, special, someone who liked her for more than her looks, she reminded herself as she resisted the urge to throw his phone out of the window. 'I'm not really into one-night stands.'

'Sweet, but I wouldn't judge you, darling, and this isn't one night—we're here for the whole weekend.'

'I mean I've never had a one-night stand.'

He put down his phone. 'You've got a boyfriend?'

'Would I be here with you if I had a boyfriend?'

He pushed his glasses back on his nose, a habit that she'd always found endearing but that left her cold at that moment. 'I don't know, you know, I don't like the idea of stepping on some guy's toes... What does he do?'

'There is no guy. I don't have a boyfriend. You're my first.'

'One weekend doesn't mean we're engaged, sweetheart.'

'You're my first lover!'

He laughed at the joke, then, when she didn't join in, stopped. 'Not seriously.'

'Totally seriously.'

'But you can't be...you're a...you've always been...'

'Easy?' She read the expression in his eyes before he looked away and the cold ache in her chest intensified.

At her sides her fingers flexed as she fought the urge to bring her arms up in a protective gesture across her chest. It was pride that kept her chin at a challenging angle while inside she had shrivelled up in shame and embarrassment.

'No. It's just, you have to admit, you came on to me like—and Ben in Marketing...he says...'

'What does Ben in Marketing say?'

It finally dawned on him that she was serious and he looked sick. 'Oh, God, Lara, I don't do virgins, hell, no! It's such a responsibility. This is just a bit of fun, and when Carol had to cancel I couldn't get a refund.'

'Carol?'

'You wouldn't know her. She doesn't have to work, she's my, my…well, we're not actually engaged yet but—'

'So when your fiancée couldn't make it you looked around for someone who everyone knows is an easy lay…'

His sulky pout vanished as he cut across her. 'Well, you weren't supposed to be a bloody virgin!'

'So sorry, my mistake, but that's the problem with small print, isn't it?' she commiserated. 'How about if I go away, get some scalps under my belt, and come back? Will that change things?'

'We-e-ell…'

Unbelievable! He was actually considering it! She edged her voice with ice as she ground out, 'I wouldn't sleep with you if you came with a seat on the board.'

If they were handing out awards for sheer blind stupidity, I, Lara reflected grimly, *would have had a clean sweep.*

'Oh, and I doubt that rich, doesn't-have-to-work Carol would have been impressed by the room.' *A cheater and a cheapskate, Lara, you know how to pick them!*

As she went over the scene yet again, wincing at her exit line, her tears dried and she realised that, not only did she have no idea where she was, but when she had made her dramatic exit she had taken nothing with her, not her purse, her phone…nothing.

She paused and looked around her, debating her options. She could continue to wander aimlessly feeling sorry for herself, try to retrace her steps or find someone and ask for directions back to the hotel. Option three made the most sense, but the street was deserted.

A moment later, she wished the street had stayed deserted as out of a side alley a group of young men appeared, five or six of them making enough noise for twenty. There was some good-natured banter and a bit of pushing and shoving.

It was hard to tell the mood and quite honestly she didn't fancy staying around to find out.

Alcohol, testosterone, peer pressure—not a good combination.

Hampered by her high spiky heels, she only got a few steps before one of the group spotted her.

Lara didn't react to him or to the cacophony of calls and whistles, and instead just carried on walking. *Do not show fear! Do not show fear!*

Any minute now someone would walk round that corner, a figure of authority, someone who would say… 'Ouch!'

By some miracle she managed not to fall when one of her heels came clear off, but her recovery was not elegant and the pain that shot through her ankle was agonising. She registered the laughter behind and this time it was her temper, not her heel, that snapped.

In the grip of a red-mist moment, she slipped off the broken shoe and, with it in her hand, turned to face the group. Her chest lifted in tune with her angry inhalations, her green eyes flashing contempt and fury, her mind clear of the fear she had felt just moments ago. The group of young men became the focus of all her accumulated anger and the humiliation seething inside her.

She was so focused on them that the fact that someone *had* come around the corner didn't register on Lara's radar.

Her red hair swirled around her like a silken curtain as she allowed her eyes to travel disdainfully over their collective heads.

Wrath swelled inside her, mingled with self-disgust. She had been running from them, and they were just kids… Well, teenagers really. Although this did not entirely remove the potential threat they represented, Lara was too mad to care. This was the real Lara, the one who stood her ground, not the one who'd run off crying because her dream lover had turned out to be a totally useless louse.

She took several limping steps towards them. Nobody was laughing now, the victim having taken them all by surprise, or perhaps they were just stunned by her beauty.

The scene's new onlooker could identify with that!

Dio, but she was utterly stunning! She managed by some miracle to be graceful, even minus one heel. The red dress she wore clung lovingly to every inch of her sinuous curves and clashed with the glorious cloud of hair she tossed back.

She brandished the shoe in one hand while delivering a killer glare at her persecutors like some glorious Valkyrie descended from the heavens. And then Raoul got his first full look at her face.

The purity of her features had been visible in profile—she had a little chin, high forehead, smooth sculpted cheeks, and straight little nose. But what he hadn't been able to appreciate fully was the liquid flash of incredible long-lashed eyes set beneath curved, feathery, dark brows or the miracle of her mouth, the firm bottom lip softened by the lush fullness of the upper.

If the first stroke of heat had nailed him to the spot, this subsequent one shut down his brain, though the absence of his higher functions did not prevent other parts of his body continuing to act and react with painful independence.

'Your idea of a good night out, is it?'

English, her voice pitched low even in anger; it had a sexy huskiness as she rounded on the gang who probably didn't understand a word she was saying.

One laughed and she pounced on him with the verbal punch of a spitting cat. 'Big man, aren't you, with your friends around you?' she jeered, swinging her stabbing finger around the group.

'Alone would you or any of your friends here be so brave? You're a bunch of pathetic losers who should be ashamed of themselves...' She focused on the ringleader and pointed the finger at him. 'If I was your mother I'd be ashamed!'

Under the battering tirade, several of the boys started to back away and one even lifted his hand and said, 'Sorry, beautiful lady.'

Raoul agreed with the description but would have added gutsy to the description. He couldn't think of another woman he knew who would have handled the situation in the same way. It had been a risky move, but you couldn't help admire her bloody-minded bravery.

Who was she, this brave, slightly crazy red-head? She bent to rub her ankle, causing the red dress to pull tight across her hips and behind.

He thought that must be the trigger, her lovely bottom, and raging teenage hormones. What-ever the cause, the effect was an immediate and complete change of atmosphere. One second it looked as though the situation had been defused, but then one boy—that was all it ever took—who clearly wanted to show off in front of his friends, took a swaggering step forward. He yelled out a mocking taunt at his retreating comrades and advanced towards the redhead with leering intent.

As he watched, Raoul's jaw tightened, though he could tell the girl didn't understand a word of the filth the kid flung at her, but his attitude needed no translation. She stood poised in a flight-or-fight mode, watching him like a lamb watching a fox.

The situation, he decided, had gone on long enough. Raoul stepped out of the shadows, fists clenched. He found there was a smile on his face, now he finally had a legitimate target for the anger that still swirled around inside him.

Lara's energising burst of angry adrenaline had exploded like a courageous firework, but now that it had smouldered and faded away she felt scared and terrifyingly vulnerable as the boy moved towards her.

She wanted to run but her feet seemed nailed to the ground. In the periphery of her vision she was aware that the others had stopped walking away, a couple had turned back and they were all watching...waiting...?

Weirdly her brain carried on functioning regardless of the paralysing dread. Then as the paralysis lifted instinct took over and she moved towards one of the street lights. An illusion of safety was better than nothing.

She lifted her hand to her ear and began to speak, her clear voice floating across to the young men, confusing them for a moment. But then one noticed that she had no phone in her hand and the yells began again.

Do not show fear.

A bit late for that, Lara thought. The group had slowly moved until she was surrounded. *You should have run when you had the chance*, said the voice in her head. Too late now! One tormentor might not have been so bad. She could have dealt with one, talked her way out perhaps, but with several, all egging each other on...?

Aware that her options had been reduced to calling for help and hoping someone would come to her aid, Lara opened her mouth to shout. Only a strangled squeak emerged, but it was drowned out by a new voice, a voice that held an edge of bored irritation.

'Where have you been? I said outside the casino!'

The youths stopped and swivelled towards him. Raoul raised a sardonic brow and allowed his disdainful glance to drift over them, satisfied they were not going to present a problem. He ignored the flicker of something close to regret—now was not the time to get his knuckles bloody—and instead turned his scrutiny to the luscious redhead. As their glances connected he saw comprehension supplant the shock in her wide-spaced eyes—could that colour possibly be real?—and she didn't miss a beat before replying, 'Casino…?' She shook her head. 'No, you said we'd go on there afterwards.'

And *that* smile…!

He'd never understood dedicated enthusiasts who waited for hours in often uncomfortable positions to catch a glimpse of a rare bird. But he would wait for ever to see that smile again, especially as it deepened, revealing a dimple in her smooth cheek. Raoul couldn't think of a reason in the world not to respond to the challenge in her emerald eyes.

'And I'm not late, you're early.'

He watched as she pulled off her other shoe, giving another excellent view of her delicious bottom, and strolled with a sexy sway of her hips towards him. 'Luckily for you,' she breathed, 'I'm very understanding.' *What are you doing, Lara?*

God knows! came the answer, but it felt…what? Actually it was hard to put a label on the fizz in her blood. The nearest she could liken it to was champagne bubbles bursting, vastly preferable to feeling like some silly little girl who had run away.

No, you're just a silly girl who is jumping from the frying pan into the fire! It seems you're not content with laughing at the face of danger—you have to set a collision course with it!

The racing thoughts slid through her head in the time it took her to fully absorb the man who had decided to be her guardian angel. Not that there was anything angelic about him, unless you were talking the dark, fallen and supremely sexy variety! Her first glance had told her that and even with several feet separating them she had felt the impact on her senses of the sensuality he projected, raw and primal.

A little shudder traced a path down her spine as she realised this wasn't a case of someone trying to be something—he *was* something. There was nothing contrived about the maleness, it was simply an integral part of him.

The powerful sexual charge he oozed made it almost irrelevant that he was the best-looking man she had ever seen. Well, not *quite* irrelevant, she admitted as her eyes travelled the long, lean length of him.

He was tall, *very* tall with the broad-of-shoulder, lean-of-hip sort of muscular frame usually associated with athletes. He was dressed expensively in a black suit, and a tie of the same colour was looped around his open-necked shirt; the vee of skin it revealed showed the same glowing golden tone as his face, minus the stubble that dusted his jaw and lean cheeks.

The stubble was the same black as his brows, which were straight and thick, one angled in at a sardonic slant above the narrow, heavy-lidded, thickly lashed eyes they framed. His strong-boned face was a miraculous arrangement of planes and angles, razor-edged high cheekbones, high forehead, aquiline nose and a strong jaw.

The only thing that alleviated the overwhelming masculinity was his mouth and the sensual fullness of his lower lip, though any suggestion of softness was counterbalanced by his firm upper lip, which had a hint of cruelty about it.

Her rescuer was doing some looking himself, his expression shielded by his heavy eyelids, but when he reached her bare feet one dark brow hitched higher.

Lara felt a giggle well up in her throat.

Up to that point he'd been making an effort to retain what grip on reality he had left, but the seductive sound she made precluded any return of common sense. He felt as hot as the glorious waves of her hair looked, and it was all he could do not to reach out and touch the flames.

'Long story.' She lowered her voice and leaned in closer, placing her hands on his forearms to steady herself. As her fingers pressed through the fabric she could feel the hard, sinewy strength beneath, and her stomach muscles quivered. 'Would thank you be premature? Are they still there?' she whispered.

'A couple.'

Lara wanted to ask how he knew when he'd not taken his eyes off her face, but she couldn't. Her throat was full, not with tears, but with something else, the same something that was sending intermittent tremors through her body.

They were standing close enough to be taken for lovers, close enough for his nostrils to quiver in response to the scent of her hair. He fought the primitive compulsion to pull her into him, let her feel what she was doing to him.

'You saved me.'

'It was a pleasure,' he said, breathing in that scent.

The corners of her mouth lifted in a rueful grimace. 'I didn't handle it very well.'

He watched her smooth brow furrow. There was something quite fascinating about the expressions that flickered across her vivid little face.

'I lost my temper.' She bit her lip and tilted her head downwards, looking up at him through the mesh of her lashes. 'It's been a…not good day.'

'I've had one of those too.'

It was a connection. The silence could have been companionable, but it wasn't. The air was charged with a sexual tension so thick that Lara struggled to breathe. She'd never experienced anything like this before.

'Have I said thank you?'

His dark eyes smiled, the crinkles at the corners deepening. 'My money was on you.'

'I was scared stiff.' She gave a tiny shudder. 'Well, thank you anyway…?'

'Raoul. Raoul Di Vittorio.'

'Thank you, Raoul. I'm Lara—Lara Gray.' Ignoring the voice in her head that warned she was playing with fire, she tipped her head back; hooking one hand behind his head and stretching up, she brushed his mouth with her soft, pouting lips.

She was about to pull back when his mouth began to move slowly and sensuously over her lips. She kissed him back, not teasingly now, but with a hungry longing she hadn't felt before. A moan drifted up from her throat as his tongue slid deeper. Afraid she would fall, even more afraid that this would stop, she clutched at his jacket and hung on.

When they broke apart the street was empty.

Lara stood there, gasping for air like someone who'd just run a marathon.

There were so many alarm bells ringing in his head that Raoul could barely hear himself think. What the hell was he doing?

He was forgetting.

He took hold of her hands, releasing the lapels of his jacket from her death grip. As she let go and stepped away from him her face lifted. Her lips, swollen from his kisses, quivered as she ran the tip of her tongue over them and blinked like a sleepwalker on waking somewhere unexpected.

'Oh, my!' she whispered.

The visceral stab of lust that lanced through him took Raoul's breath away. *Dio*, but she was beautiful, and he wanted to taste her again, he wanted to do a lot more than taste her.

Lara stared up at him wanting him to kiss her again, willing him to kiss her again. It was hard to escape the bold, sensual glittering in his deepset eyes, but Lara didn't even try.

The warm, heavy, dreamy sensation that held her rooted to the spot was now being supplanted by a heart-racing excitement that left her dizzy. Her stomach muscles quivered as her eyes lingered on his mouth. She couldn't tear her eyes clear of the sensually sculpted outline, nor forget the taste of brandy in his kiss.

'Are you drunk?' she asked, struggling to think through the sexual fog in her brain as she tilted her head to one side. She'd have liked to think it would matter if he was, but she'd never run full tilt into a solid wall of lust before, so the whole experience was new for her.

His mouth quirked, one corner lifting in a way she found utterly fascinating. Actually, everything about him fascinated her. She had no idea what it was she was feeling. It was visceral in a way that went beyond anything she had ever felt before.

'Not strictly sober, but not drunk.' It was, he realised, true. 'How about you?'

She shook her head, the excitement fizzing through her blood more intoxicating than champagne. 'Are you married?'

His expression didn't change but she saw something unidentifiable move in his eyes before he responded, 'Not any more.'

She reacted to his comment with a small grunt of satisfaction as the tiny furrow between her brows smoothed out. 'That's good.'

He smiled again and Lara's knees started to shake. None of this made any sense. She had planned on being seduced tonight but at no stage had she planned on not being in charge of the process. Or of being seduced by a total stranger!

'You're very beautiful.'

The faint rasp in the smooth, dark-chocolate purr of his voice made her shiver; the touch of his finger on her cheek made her insides dissolve.

'So they tell me.' His stare was hypnotic; the sensory overload was making her light-headed.

She turned her head, not enough to break the connection. 'This is quite mad.'

'Mad can be good.'

'Can it?'

His dark eyes gleamed. 'Oh, yes.' The furrow between his dark brows deepened. 'Where did you come from?' he asked, continuing to stroke her cheek.

'I'm not sure.'

'You just dropped from heaven.' No angel had a mouth like hers. He focused on her lips and the pain in his groin, not the deeper pain that cut up his insides. She was an oasis to escape that pain, to lose it and himself inside.

His thumb touched the pouting curve of her lower lip and his hand stilled. 'Boyfriend?'

Her chin lifted a notch, her nostrils flaring as her green eyes sparked. 'Not any more,' she rebutted firmly.

'Where are you going?'

She closed a door in her head, blotting out Mark's rejection and her stupidity.

'With you, I hope.' She heard the words, the supremely confident tone, even though inside she was anything but. Inside, she was holding her breath. She'd only just picked herself up and now she'd set herself up for another fall.

Head thrown back, she fixed him with an emerald stare that sent a fresh flash of heat through his already primed body. He could feel the hairs on the nape of his neck tingle as his body hardened in anticipation. Another time he might have blocked out his primitive response to this woman, might have heard the alarm bells, but tonight he didn't think beyond it, instead he embraced the mindlessness of it.

For the first time since he'd discovered Jamie's body he wasn't hearing Rob's broken voice in his head sobbing, 'What am I going to do without him? He's gone *for ever*. He's gone…gone… gone…for ever…for *ever*, Raoul.'

That was what he had kept repeating over and over until Raoul could feel nothing but pain, his, Rob's, just a universe of pain that went on and on.

Now he was feeling something that wasn't pain and regret, and it didn't matter that it was shallow or transient. He needed breathing space— not that he could *breathe* when he looked at this woman.

Did the ability to think of sex while in the

depths of grief make him shallow? If Jamie had been burying him, would his brother have been able to escape so easily? Would he have wanted to?

He pushed away the speculation, the grief, the anger, the loss and lost himself to the moment of this intoxicatingly beautiful woman in his arms. He looked down into her sensual face and released a slow sigh. If he'd believed in fate, if he'd believed there was actually some grand plan, he'd have thought fate had sent her there at that moment.

He didn't believe in fate but he did believe in embracing opportunities when they appeared, and the thought of shutting out the blackness in this woman's arms just for an hour or two was irresistible.

'That works for me, *cara*.'

She felt a rush of relief—for a moment she'd thought he'd been going to say thanks but no, thanks. Her confidence had already taken a battering today.

'Good.'

He laughed, the sound sending a fresh tingle of excitement through her.

'I've never met anyone quite like you.'

'I have an identical twin sister.'

He slung a teasing look over his shoulder. 'Is she around?'

If she were she wouldn't be doing this with you. The thought came with an unbidden image of their headmistress berating her for some minor infringement 'People will not respect you, Lara, unless you respect yourself. Your sister would never—'

'No, she isn't.'

Her flat response drew a sardonic look. 'I was joking.'

For a split second as their eyes locked, Raoul thought he glimpsed a vulnerability that did not belong to the self-possessed, sensual creature who stood in front of him. But a moment later it was gone.

It had probably never been there.

Hell, he was *not* going to talk himself out of this. From the corner of his eye he saw a taxi and lifted his hand. His place was within walking distance but prolonging this agony was not on his agenda.

It was happening so quickly, she had no time to think; was this a good thing or a bad thing?

She didn't know and didn't want to—the answer might make her walk away.

And she didn't want to…she *really* didn't want to.

Her senses were strangely heightened and yet she felt distanced from what was happening as a taxi stopped and then with the snap of the door she was inside, the jarring noise introducing a sense of reality to her dreamlike state.

But this was no dream.

CHAPTER THREE

'IS SOMETHING WRONG?'

Lara shook her head and her spurt of panic subsided. Instead, desire, warm and fluid, spread through her body as his iron-hard thigh nudged hers, then a second later drew away.

'Is it your ankle?'

'My ankle?' It took her a moment to recall turning it earlier. The pain had been sharp but it had subsided now. 'No, it's fine, see?' Proving her point, she hitched the long skirt of her dress slightly to expose her calf and foot, stretching them out as far as the confined space allowed. 'I just turned it, but it's fine now.'

She turned her head and found his eyes on her leg. She could see a nerve relaxing and tensing like a ticking bomb in his lean cheek as he stared.

He turned his head, his eyes only brushing hers for a moment before he leaned forward to give the driver directions in Italian. But one glimpse of the devouring heat in them was enough to pull

her back in her seat shaking, frightened not by
the intent she had seen written in his face but the
response it had awoken in her.

She sat there, thinking of the taste of his cool,
firm mouth, her hand pressed tight to her quivering stomach.

Raoul didn't move any closer or attempt to put
his arm around her. As the car drew away from
the kerb they could have been strangers forced
to share a space on crowded public transport...
except for the air thick with possibility between
them.

Lara's head was spinning as she sat there, and
her thoughts began racing to keep pace with the
turbulent thud of her heart.

*What are you doing, Lara? You have no idea
where you are, let alone where you are going.
You just got into a car with a total stranger, and
the plan is to have sex with him?*

*Mark thought you were easy—how is this dif-
ferent?*

What does it matter? Lara asked herself.
She was just using him. It would be liberating;
she wouldn't have to pretend. So far her wild-
child reputation had been window dressing. This
was real.

A conversation with her recently engaged friend, Jane, surfaced in her head. A crowd of them had been sitting in a bar drinking shots, except for Lara, the designated driver with a zero tolerance to alcohol, while Jane showed off her ring.

'It was magic, guys, the moment I saw him I was dizzy with longing—you know what I mean?'

Because it was expected Lara had smiled and nodded her agreement along with everyone else, but she hadn't known what Jane meant. Not really. And she had actually been happy in her ignorance. Losing your balance, not to mention your grip on reality—Jane's dream man was not exactly what you'd call irresistible—was not something she envied anyone.

Had she lost her grip on reality now? It wasn't too late to change her mind.

She halted the inner dialogue and turned her head. Raoul was sitting back, both hands rested on his thighs, as he looked straight ahead. She sensed a darkness in him, and in profile the austere beauty of his face brought a lump of emotion to her throat.

He's not a sunset, or an ocean view, she reminded herself. *He's a man, a stranger. And you're in the back of a taxi with him.*

'I can take you to your hotel, if you prefer.'

The offer made her relax. The option was there, although she knew it was one she had no intention of taking. 'No, I don't want that. I want you.'

She heard a sharp intake of breath but his only response was a jerky movement of his dark head.

Raoul didn't trust himself to touch her, because he knew that when he did he wouldn't be able to let her go. The scent of her, the warmth where their thighs were almost touching, were driving him insane. A woman had not made him feel this way in a long time.

He had never been so relieved for a journey to end.

'We're here.'

Standing beside him on the pavement, watching him pay off the cab, Lara wondered where *here* was. There were no names, numbers or signs on any of the anonymous buildings this side of the street, though she could just make out a plaque on a building opposite. Squinting, she read *Embassy*, then before she could read the rest of the inscription a big set of gates slid silently open.

He gestured for her to go through, which after a tiny pause she did.

Nothing in the street suggested that this place existed.

'It's beautiful.'

Her apprehension gave way to appreciation as the tall gates closed, cutting them off from the street again. The softly lit courtyard they stood in was stone cobbled, uneven and old. The plants that spilled from the massed stone troughs in the central section filled the air with the heady scents of jasmine and lavender, and water spilled from a stone lion's head set in the wall out into an ornamental pool.

She tilted her head back. The building that enclosed the space on three sides was tall, the first-floor windows arranged symmetrically with wrought-iron Juliet balconies.

'Is it a hotel?'

He shook his head. 'No, I live here.'

'Alone?' The possibility seemed extraordinary to Lara. It was a massive place for one person... had he got the marital home after the divorce? Assuming there had been a divorce—really she knew nothing about him. She exhaled a measured sigh, starting slightly when he placed a hand be-

tween her shoulder blades. The touch of his fingers on her bare skin made her gasp.

'This way.'

Quivering inside with anticipation that she struggled to hide beneath an air of cheerful insouciance, she let him guide her up a small flight of shallow stone steps, as though she were in the habit of doing this sort of thing every day of the week.

He leaned across her to put a key in the lock of the heavy metal-banded door that was dark with age. Given the traditional, almost historical, external appearance of the building, the inside caused her to gasp in surprise.

Internally it had been opened up—presumably walls had been knocked down to create this one massive ground-floor space, bisected by a staircase that seemed to float in mid-air. The end wall had been taken out and was now glass; several sections of internal wall were exposed stone while others were pale limewashed.

The furniture was eclectic. Big, comfortable-looking sofas, a long, highly polished antique trestle table, and one entire wall lined with floor-to-ceiling bookshelves.

They had entered the kitchen area, which

boasted every modern appliance set in pale ash units with polished stone work surfaces.

'This is not what I expected.' But then, nothing about their encounter had been.

Raoul gave the space a dismissive glance. He felt no emotional connection to it; he'd simply given the architect free rein. The place said nothing about him or his taste in books, except that he liked big spaces. It wasn't the soundest of financial investments he'd ever made—he'd bought it for its location and size, only to discover it was falling down.

'The place was riddled with wet rot, dry rot, deathwatch beetle, I could go on... A lesson in the danger of buying without a structural survey. Once the building was made safe I had to decide whether to reinstate the original period features or not.' His shoulders lifted.

'And you chose not.'

He nodded.

'It's spectacular.' She clamped her lips together to prevent a gushing response.

He took a step closer and the room got smaller, her heartbeat got faster, and there seemed a strong possibility her shaking knees were going to fold.

'I always talk a lot when I'm nervous.' Should she tell him before…?

Oh, yeah, because that worked so well last time.

'You're nervous?'

'Well, this might surprise you,' she said, forcing a laugh, 'but this isn't something I do every day.'

His dark brows lifted. 'No, it doesn't surprise me. Why should it?'

'It's just—'

'You don't have to explain.'

She felt hot as embarrassed colour flew to her cheeks. 'No…no, of course not.' *The man doesn't want your life history, Lara, he wants sex.*

He watched the blush and recognised the vulnerability it exposed. His jaw clenched. He didn't want vulnerable, he wanted hot, mind-numbing sex with a beautiful, bold, confident woman who could fearlessly face down a gang of thugs.

Where had she gone?

He heaved a resigned sigh and swallowed his growing frustration. The hot-cold thing was killing him and the prospect of a night of cold showers did not appeal, but in such a matter acceptance was the only recourse.

'Would you like a coffee…?'

Lara swallowed but didn't dodge his stare. There was probably something playful she should say but the emotions in her throat made even the basic truth hard to utter.

'We both know I don't want a coffee.'

'I *thought* I did. What do you want?' He lifted a strand of her shining hair with one finger and let it fall. 'Is that real?'

'Everything about me is real.' *Good line, Lara. Means nothing, but good line!* 'And I want you.'

She didn't attempt to escape his gleaming stare. She quivered as he cupped her face with one hand, her eyelashes lowered and falling in a dark filigree against her cheek. They lifted a moment later when his free hand curved possessively around her bottom.

A soft moan left her parted lips as with barely leashed violence he pulled her in hard against him.

'*That* is real,' he ground out, his breath warm on her face as he caught the soft flesh of her lower lip between his teeth. 'What you do to me is real. Everything about you,' he slurred, bending his head to move his lips over the pulse spot at the base of her throat, 'is real.'

When was the last time that he had experienced

anything close to the primitive need to possess that was pounding through him at that moment? It was madness!

But madness had never felt so sweet and as the passion between them escalated definitions became irrelevant.

The kiss seemed to go on for ever. Lara gave herself up to it and the dormant passion deep inside her that he had awoken. Her head was spinning and instinctively she wound her slim arms tight around his neck, and met the repeated probing thrust of his tongue with an eagerness that masked her inexperience.

She gave a little gasp of shock as his hand moved up to cover one breast, his thumb brushing the swollen peak through the red silky fabric, causing the gasp to slide seamlessly into a low guttural moan of pleasure.

He lifted his head to look into her passion-glazed eyes, then he moved his hips against her. He watched her eyes darken in instant response, then slid his hand up and down the long smooth lines of her thigh. He heard her breath quicken before, with a muffled cry, she jumped into him, wrapping her long legs around his waist.

Raoul caught her, and brushed the hair from

her face to expose one side of her neck before spreading his hands supportively under her bottom and kissing the smooth swanlike curve he had revealed. He began to carry her towards the staircase.

'I never knew that anything could feel this good, this *right*.'

She didn't know that she had voiced her thoughts out loud until his fingers slid around her jaw, forcing her face up to him.

'Don't stop!'

The fierce intentness of his dark stare did not soften as he gave a short, hard laugh. It was all he could do not to back her against the wall and take her there and then, but this was too good to hurry, much too good. 'I have no intention of stopping, *cara*,' he admitted thickly.

The need to define or analyse what was happening had passed. She tasted sweet as again he drove his tongue with sensual precision between her plump, parted lips.

Like a drowning man he kissed her as he walked with her in his arms towards the bedroom door.

Lara had a hazy impression of cool as he carried her across the room to the low platform bed set centre stage. But the pulse of need inside her left little room for anything else. It was a need she couldn't explain even if she'd wanted to—all she wanted was him.

'I want you so much it hurts.'

He growled a response in Italian, the urgency of that language making more sense to Lara than his words as he laid her down on the bed, sweeping the pillows out of the way as he did so.

He was above her, his face a dark blur as he lowered himself. The hard press of his arousal, as it ground into her belly for a moment before he rolled them both to one side, drew a low, feral-sounding groan from Lara's lips. The erotic contact offered deep pleasure, but no release for the ache of her own arousal, the throbbing need between her legs.

As they lay thigh to thigh there was a tremor in the big hand he lifted to curve around her face, turning it up to him until their eyes caught. Hungrily he took in the details of her passion-flushed skin.

He felt something tighten in his chest as he stared into her luminous green eyes, which were glazed with passion; her plump lips were soft, trembling, almost vulnerable. His gaze remained locked on to hers as he kissed her cheeks, his warm breath moving over the downy softness until he found her mouth and possessed it before he levered himself away and began to rip off his clothes.

Watching him through half-closed eyes, Lara wondered if she ought to be undressing too. The question was academic, as her body was infiltrated by a heavy languor that seemed to pin her to the bed. She watched him, her breathing getting ragged, until finally he stood there naked, like a tall, aroused god.

Her breath caught, hot excitement flooded her body and a scalding wave of heat tinged her skin with a delicate pink. He was beautiful, and aroused—*very* aroused—a fact that was hard to escape!

Looking at his arousal made her very aware of her own. The idea of her hands framing him, her body holding him, made her ache in a way she had never experienced. He strode back to the bed and dropped down on his knees beside it.

'I love your mouth.' An expression of rapt fascination on her face, she reached up and trailed her fingers down his stubbled cheek.

Raoul caught her wrist; turning her hand palm

up towards his mouth, he felt her shiver as he pressed a fierce, damp kiss to her wrist. He ran his fingers down the smooth skin of her shoulder, hooking the shoestring strap of her dress down as he did so. Then, sliding his finger under the folds of red silk that were cut to form a soft cowl neckline, he exposed one perfect breast. Raoul reached out, his touch almost reverent as he cupped the quivering mound, weighing it for a moment, then with a groan he bent his head.

The sensation of his mouth on her skin was a sharp, searing pleasure; her body arched in response. She barely registered him peeling the second strap from her shoulders as she held his dark head, her fingers deep in his thick hair.

When he lifted his head he looked at her with eyes that seemed to burn from within. The rigid control he exerted drew the skin taut across the bones of his face, emphasising the dramatic bone structure.

His kiss, when it came, was deep and plundering, the seething emotions inside her burning hotter as she kissed him back, making tiny mewling noises of pleasure in her throat as he came to lie beside her.

The first skin-to-skin contact as he pulled her

against him made her gasp, her nerve endings quivering as her breasts were crushed against his chest.

She ran her hands over the hard muscles of his shoulders, pulling back a little as she moved down his chest. His skin was warm, slightly damp, and, when she bent her head to taste, it was salty. She pulled herself half over him, running her hands over his body, getting bolder as she drew moans and gasps from him.

She bent her face to his belly and followed the line her finger had just traced with her tongue. 'Mmm...' Her murmur turned into a soft squeal as he tugged her dress down over her hips.

A couple of wriggles and a moment later she was lying there in just a pair of silky, French-cut pants. No longer lying on top of him, she was on her back, one leg anchored to the bed by his muscular, hair-roughened thigh.

Her nerve endings reacted to the brush of his eyes as they would his touch.

But then, the unexpected gentleness as he kissed her lips softly made her chest tighten with emotion.

She touched his face and whispered his name. Raoul's nostrils flared as he bent his head, but this time the kiss was not soft. It was hard and demanding, bruising in its intensity. He kissed her as if he'd drain her, and everything he wanted to take, Lara wanted to give, and more.

Her fingertips dug into the golden skin of his back as they kissed, her body felt fluid and on fire, but when she felt his fingers slide under the lacy edge of her panties she tensed. Feeling his eyes on her face through her closed lids, she blinked them open.

'Relax.'

She smiled faintly, then breathed a tremulous sigh that was lost in the moisture of his mouth.

She moved against his hand as he touched her through the silk, and closed her eyes, focusing on the sensation. Then as his fingers moved under the silk across the damp folds of sensitised skin Lara forgot to breathe, forgot her name; the pleasure was mindless and all-consuming. She dug her teeth into her lower lip as he slid her panties down her legs with what felt like tantalising slowness.

When he nudged her thighs with his knee she parted them with a sigh of relief.

'I can't stand it.'

Her agonised whisper drew a deep groan from

Raoul, who caught her wrists onto the pillow either side of her face. His chest heaved as he lowered himself down, fighting the almost overwhelming compulsion to possess her fully in one thrust.

The strain of fighting himself showed in his glistening face as he entered her, the knowledge that he had never wanted a woman this much before locked away for another time.

Lara had been expecting some discomfort. What she hadn't expected was to be overcome by a climax almost before her body had adjusted to the sensation of him inside her.

It rocked her as every muscle clenched around him. A low keening cry was wrenched from her throat, and the waves of intense, mind-blowing pleasure just went on and on. She was so focused on what was happening to her that she didn't immediately realise it wasn't happening for him. Before she could come back down to earth he was moving again, pushing deeper into her with each thrust.

Lara's hips arched up to meet him, she could feel all of him and all of her, and the cell-deep awareness was almost painful, like some bright, beautiful light. Eyes squeezed tight in an effort to fully appreciate each individual sensation, Lara clung on because she didn't know what else to do. Everything that was happening was new and wonderful. Her focus narrowed until her entire world consisted of just moving with him, flowing into him.

The heat between them became a furnace as he reached deep into her. Just as Lara began to feel that she could not bear it, the invisible wall melted and it happened again, only this time it was even more intense—her body convulsed by a series of deep contractions until every nerve ending vibrated with pleasure. She actually saw starbursts through the paper-thin skin of her eyelids, and then as the tensions left her body in a series of juddering jolts she heard him groan and felt the heat of his release.

'You're beautiful.' His voice cracked as he bent his head down to her, his nose brushing hers as he angled a kiss across her lips, before rolling away.

CHAPTER FOUR

STILL FLOATING, Lara opened her eyes. His bedroom was a monochrome blur, pale walls, dark
furniture, a painting on one wall that appeared
to be just a splash of red. She turned her head
towards the breeze blowing in through three
windows that reached the floor, the transparent
drapes fluttering and billowing in the breeze.

If she turned her head the other way she'd see
Raoul. She could hear him breathing hard, almost as hard as she was.

She turned her head the other way.

Raoul's eyes were closed, and his chest was
lifting as he breathed in and out, the golden skin
glistening under a layer of moisture. In profile
his face had an austere quality, like a statue. His
passion-sated body continued to exert a strong
fascination for Lara; the strength, the hardness,
the contrast between them was part of that fascination. He was in every way a physical male

ideal—*her* ideal certainly—from his lean musculature to his long limbs.

She had experienced so much with him. For a time they had been two parts of one whole and yet now they were separate—worlds apart.

Lara suddenly felt sad, and she didn't know why.

He was lying with one arm curved above his head, and without opening his eyes he lowered it. She wanted to hang on to the perfect golden moment but all the questions she didn't want to think about popped into her head.

What would he say?

What should she say?

The sheet lay in a tangled heap between them. She hooked her toe in it and pulled, and had managed to drag a section halfway up her legs when she realised he was watching her.

'Are you cold?' Without waiting for a reply he reached for her, pulling her into his arms.

She lay stiff for a moment and then relaxed against him, tucking her head against his shoulder. Raoul stroked a hand down the smooth curve of her back, enjoying the satiny texture.

He had enjoyed her.

He'd enjoyed many women, he enjoyed sex, but

it had been the most erotic experience in his life and she'd been a virgin.

Should he feel bad about that?

If he was honest, the knowledge, when he had realised, had obviously been staggering but had also been a massive turn-on. He supposed it was programmed into male genes, a hangover from less enlightened times, primitive man claiming his mate.

The theory did offer an explanation for the explosive surge of possessiveness he'd experienced when she'd nestled in his arms.

Bleakness filtered into his dark eyes. It would pass—most things did.

Before the dark thought claimed him she moved, snuggling in deeper, a slim arm snaking across his middle to anchor herself. She was half asleep already. Once more he felt a tightening in his chest, something breaking free that came perilously close to tenderness. He watched her eyelids, heavy with lashes that lay on her cheek like butterfly wings—she was sound asleep.

Another situation that he was not used to. Raoul could not remember the last time he'd slept with a woman in his own bed, and as for actually sleeping…that was easy. Never, not once, since the early months of his marriage.

Raoul closed his eyes. He had been functioning on a couple of hours a night since Jamie's death. It had reached the point where he didn't want to fall asleep, knowing that he'd relive the moment he found Jamie in his dreams, the images twisted and warped. He'd jerk awake in a cold sweat, the panic in his belly trying to claw its way out.

Tonight he didn't dream at all, so it was a shock to be woken so abruptly.

Raoul was jolted into wakefulness by an ear-piercing scream. Beside him, Lara was sitting upright, her eyes wide, staring and unfocused. As he raised himself up on his elbow she turned her head and blinked several times.

'You had a nightmare.'

'Did I?' She gave him a wide-eyed-kitten look.

'You don't remember?' He slid an arm over her warm, bare shoulder and pulled her back down.

Raoul looked into the face inches away from his, her glorious hair a wild halo, wide luminous eyes looking back at him, and he experienced a wave of fierce protectiveness that was on several levels more shocking than her scream.

'You *really* don't remember?'

'No, I never do, it's a night terror. I thought I'd grown out of them.'

'Not tonight.'

'I suppose I should have told you.'

She might have meant the night terrors but he knew she didn't.

'It might,' he agreed, 'have been an idea.'

'You...it was...thank you.' She was back on earth, not floating two feet above it, but Lara couldn't help wonder if it was the same earth... or she the same person.

There you go again, Lara—dramatising. It was sex, not an entry into an alternative dimension. People did it every day.

Of their own volition her eyes slid down his body; the light duvet that now covered them both reached his narrow hips, revealing the golden-toned skin of his flat, ridged belly and broad, powerful chest and shoulders.

The earthy image made her shudder. Her stomach muscles clenched, a stronger version of the delicious little aftershocks that had come in the wake of the crashing release.

'I know a good cure for insomnia.' And the darkness in his heart, which he felt receding.

She flashed a mock-innocent smile while inside her heart was hammering wildly. For the first time in her life she understood why people did crazy things for sex. 'A glass of milk?'

Her smile made him hot. 'You taste more of strawberries and cream.' His mouth remaining a fraction of an inch from hers, he whispered throatily, 'I want to touch you all over this time.' He feathered a kiss across her parted lips. 'Taste you.'

She gave a little whimper and whispered, 'Please.'

It was a plea she made several times during the next hour, as he took her to the brink several times before he finally let her fall over the edge with him.

Utterly drained, but more at peace than he had felt in a week, no, a lot, *lot* longer, he barely had the strength to roll off her before sleep claimed him. It took Lara a long time to come down from the high she was floating on, and when she did her sleep was shallow and disturbed.

He woke up to the sound of the shower in the adjoining bathroom. He had barely managed to groggily lever himself into a sitting position and drag a hand through his hair when she appeared.

Her freshly scrubbed, shiny face and wet curling hair looking incongruous against the indecently sexy red dress.

'Sorry I woke you.' The chirpy voice belonged to the red dress. 'Hope you don't mind, but I used your toothbrush.'

'You can use anything you like but keep the volume down,' he pleaded, holding his head.

'Are you hung over?' Did he even remember making love? She smiled her way through a stab of totally irrational bitterness. For her this one-night stand had been memorable, her first, but that didn't mean it had any significance for him.

'No, but I'm human,' he retorted. 'Being that cheerful in the morning,' he concluded positively, 'is not.'

'So you're not a morning person.'

The scowling lines of his staggeringly handsome face melted without warning into a wicked grin as he leaned back against the pillows, hands behind his head, and raised a mocking brow. 'There are those that might dispute that…'

Her cheeks burning, Lara lifted her chin. 'I'll take your word on that one,' she said, wondering whether he could be any more smugly self-satisfied. Even if his smugness was justified, it was an unattractive trait, and discovering a flaw in this perfect specimen made her feel slightly more cheerful as she moved across the room towards a mirror, combing her fingers through her wet curls.

Watching the gentle sway of her breasts against the red silk as she walked across the room, he felt his lust stir lazily. Actually, not so lazily.

'I have never slept with a virgin before.' And it had not been on any list of things to do in the near future.

She swivelled gracefully around, the expression on her beautiful face wary.

'You've clearly got no sexual hang-ups...' Though she did possess a delicious ability to blush. 'It's none of my business,' he conceded, 'but why?'

She stood there, poised, he suspected, on the point of telling him to go to hell, when she shrugged and pulled out a stool, sinking with a sigh and a rustle of silk onto it.

'You know, I've been asking myself just that,' she admitted with disarming candour. 'I planned to lose my virginity last night, just not with you. I never really thought that casual sex would work for me without the emotional stuff, you know—

liking, a connection…but it did quite beautifully, thank you.'

'*Liking*…not love?'

Her candid gaze slid away as she got to her feet. 'I think we communicate on more of a lust level.'

'I'm assuming there is a man somewhere that came with the *emotional stuff* wondering where the hell you are.'

If it had been him, he'd have died a thousand deaths through the night imagining all the things that could have happened to her. 'What were you thinking?' he growled. 'You could have met any-one!'

'I expect Mark is asleep still.'

He reined in the surge of emotion. Sharing casual sex did not entitle him to bad-mouth a guy he didn't know, although the confirmation that he existed at all had not improved his mood, and he could think of no circumstance that excused a man allowing a woman to wander around a strange city alone at night.

'Poor guy,' he said in a voice laden with insin-cerity.

Lara missed the insincerity but heard the words, and saw a red mist.

She turned slowly, rounding on him with eyes shooting green flames.

'Poor guy,' she echoed. *'Poor guy!* He's a...' Her mouth closed over a word her mum would have been shocked her daughter even knew, and, teeth clenched, she stalked towards the bathroom.

'So you're not planning a kiss-and-make-up session.' The relief he felt was on her behalf, he told himself. Lara deserved something better.

Lara's anger faded as quickly as it had sparked into life. 'I overreacted, didn't I?' She covered her face with her hands and shook her head. 'Mark is a total and utter louse, but the situation is as much my fault as his. If I hadn't been walking around thinking I'd found my soulmate I'd have seen this coming a mile off.'

'Your hero fell off his pedestal.' It seemed suddenly sad that she would learn all too soon there were no heroes. 'So what did he do?'

She gave a laugh that rang with self-mockery and shook her head. 'Oh, why not? It's a bit of a cliché really. I came here with my boss—he asked and I said yes.

'What I *didn't* know was that I was a last-minute stand-in for his girlfriend who couldn't come, and he'd paid for the room, and he is a bit tight with money.'

It was a fault she'd been prepared to accept when he had still seemed the sensitive man of her dreams.

'It turns out he asked because he thinks I'm basically easy, actually I think he's not the only one, not that I care what people think.'

Hearing her fall back on a defence that was only used by people who *did* care, Raoul was forced to subdue a surge of protective tenderness.

'And the virgin thing,' she continued. 'I think he thought he'd been sold a...what do they call it...?'

'False bill of goods?'

She nodded. 'I said I was going to sleep with the first man I saw. I was *almost* right.'

'This boss of yours sounds like a total loser.'

'I don't know why I'm even telling you this.'

He raised a sardonic brow. 'Because I asked.' Which in itself was not just unusual and totally out of character, it was completely unheard of.

A few murmured nothings that constituted post-coital conversation were normally the precursor to him rolling out of bed and making a practised exit.

Except it was never his bed he was exiting.

From every angle this was a weird situation, almost as weird as finding he wanted to prolong this. He didn't even have a major objection to hearing her open up more, talk nonsense…maybe even contribute to that nonsense himself…?

He didn't read anything significant into it, recognising that it was not an emotional connection that was making him behave so out of character, but the knowledge that the world he had escaped from in her body last night would come rushing back the moment she vanished.

'Look, I should be going before anyone…'

He looked up and saw she was looking at a framed photo on the wall.

'That's my mother.'

'Oh!' Had she really been that obvious? 'She doesn't look Italian.' Everything about him epitomised Lara's own version of an idealised Latin male but his English was perfect and she couldn't detect any accent.

'I'm Italian on my father's side. My mother was American with a Spanish mother.' *And you are sharing this information why exactly, Raoul?* Maybe the opening-up thing was contagious?

'Your mother's dead?'

He nodded. The memory of his mother was influenced by snapshots like that one and a couple of formal portraits, which didn't match the laugh he remembered or the warm lemony scent he associated with her.

'A flu epidemic. She ought to have been safe—she wasn't an infant or elderly, she was fit and young. I was just a kid.'

An image drifted before her eyes of a boy with scratched, long brown legs and big dark eyes. Her eyes drifted of their own accord to his face, their eyes connected and something seemed to pass between them. She found the sensation so uncomfortable that she looked away quickly and changed the subject.

'Do you have such a thing as a hairdryer?' She lifted a water-darkened strand of hair. 'It takes hours to dry on its own.'

'Bottom drawer,' he said, pointing to the bathroom.

Inside the room she closed the door and, sighing, leaned back against it. Now that she didn't have to hold it together and act a version of cool, the images she had fought to banish from her head while in the room with Raoul crowded in.

Remembering the exquisite sweetness of their lovemaking was agony.

She took a deep breath and straightened her shoulders. She had been prepared for remote and maybe irritated, but not for him to be so... She shook her head. What did she know? Absolutely nothing when it came to the morning after the night before.

And this might feel awkward but she was leaving here with a lot of positives. Her first time had been with a great lover, and she had not disgraced herself by saying anything terminally stupid like, *Last night was special—it must mean something to you.*

When Lara emerged from the bathroom, her hair dried to a smooth gloss, the bedroom was filled with the aroma of fresh coffee. She followed the scent downstairs.

Raoul was standing there, coffee cup in hand, wearing a black robe loosely tied around his hips. It showed a wide vee of hard, golden, hair-roughened chest. Lara struggled to keep her eyes on his strong, angular face, which, with its dark shading of stubble, was only fractionally less disturbing.

Hauntingly beautiful. From some corner of her head the description of a hero in a novel she had read recently flashed into her head. At the time she had rolled her eyes and given up on the story midway, unable to imagine a real-life man who could be described this way, and unable to connect with the book's heroine who had walked away from a perfectly good husband to be with him.

'I cried at the end,' the friend who had recommended it had confided.

Lara hadn't cried. She'd lost patience with the heroine long before. She'd thought, *Who walks away from everything for an orgasm, no matter how bone-meltingly incredible?*

Lara hadn't known a lot about orgasms at the time, but she couldn't imagine anything that would make her give up a stable home.

And then Raoul had come into her life.

And soon he would be out again, which was good. Clean breaks were good when it came to uncomplicated sex. Actually, they were probably essential.

He put down the mug in his hand, his eyes making a sweep up from her feet to the glossy, smooth curls on her head. 'You found it, then.'

She touched her face, now clear of the last remnants of make-up from the night before. She felt naked without even a smear of lip gloss to protect her from his dark, bone-stripping stare. 'Thanks, yes.'

'Help yourself to coffee. I won't be long.'

'Thanks but I should be going.' Last night now seemed like a lifetime ago, and the rejection from Mark was a distant dream.

'I'll take you back to your hotel.'

Move on...never, ever see this man again... never touch him...never... 'No, that's—'

His voice cut across her. 'Have you got money for a taxi?'

She flushed and, gnawing on the soft fullness of her under lip, brought her lashes down in a concealing sweep.

'Exactly.'

With a flash of defiance she lifted her head, tossing back her red curls. 'I could walk.'

'And that worked out so well the last time...'

Recognising that this was a battle she wasn't about to win, Lara managed a superficial attitude of amusement as she arched a brow and asked, 'Do all your one-night stands rate taxi service?'

She was trying so hard and her pretence was painfully transparent. Raoul hid his reaction to the vulnerability he didn't want to see under an attitude of brusque impatience, and reminded himself that Lucy had once seemed sweet and vulnerable to him too.

'They do if they don't mind hanging around...' He arched a brow. 'Five minutes.'

It was only when she got in the car that she realised she'd forgotten the hotel name.

'I think it begins with a C or maybe a T and I think there was a coffee shop on the corner, no, there was definitely a coffee shop.'

'Oh, well, that makes it much easier.'

'There's no need to be sarcastic. I'm sure the name will come to me.'

When? he wondered fifteen minutes later when, naming another hotel, he got the same negative shake of her head.

'You're just confusing me now,' she accused. Bad enough that even with the top of the low-slung sports car up, in the skin-tight red dress her appearance had still elicited a lot of unwanted attention.

Raoul had advised her to ignore the horn blares and the calls from pedestrians—the Latin male seemed to have a *very* extensive non-verbal vocabulary—and then gone on to ignore his own advice, rolling down his window to react with hand signals that had never found a place into the highway code!

'I'm sure now it begins with an A…'

He audibly ground his teeth. 'I thought you'd decided it began with a T.'

'Well, a T or maybe…wait, that place there.' She hit his arm and began to bounce in her seat as she turned to look behind them. 'I remember that bar with the potted palms outside and the blue squiggly writing on the sign. Turn around… turn around…'

'We're in the middle of a one-way system. Do you mind sitting still? I'm trying to focus.' To focus on the road and not the way her breasts were trying to fight their way out of the bodice of her dress. 'Do you want me to cause a crash?'

'I don't suppose this is how you planned to spend your day.'

'*Dio mio*, do not go all humble and apologetic on me.' He found unreasonable and wilfully awkward much easier to deal with.

'It's not this way,' she said as he swung the car down an alley where the walls of the tall buildings almost touched the car on either side. To make things worse he didn't reduce his speed.

'So how well do you know Rome, then?'

She flashed him a killer look and compressed her lips.

'It was a shortcut,' she said in a quiet voice as he drew up outside the hotel.

Raoul grunted and turned his attention to the building. Like most in the area, it could have done with some TLC; he was not a person who found peeling paint picturesque. 'You're sure this is the right place?'

She nodded.

'Your boyfriend really knows how to treat a lady, doesn't he?'

'He's not my boyfriend,' she gritted.

'Has it occurred to you he might have called the police?' Her wide eyes said it hadn't.

She was thinking.

'I hope not! Well, thank you and last night... you were...kind.' With a swish of silk she left the car, her comment making him feel like a total bastard.

And maybe he was, Raoul mused as watched her walk up the steps, the sinuous sway of her body in that wicked dress causing several turned heads before she vanished inside the clapped-out-looking building.

How was the man who'd brought her here and then rejected her going to react when she appeared? Raoul knew how he'd have reacted in that position. He wasn't a possessive man, but if she'd left him and spent the night with another man he'd have throttled her, or maybe just thrown her on the bed and made love to her.

And would Lara forgive him? You never knew with women. Some were drawn like magnets to men who treated them badly.

While he was grimly contemplating make-up sex and wondering if that was what was happening, Raoul was suddenly struck by how *extreme* his reactions to this woman were. There was no middle ground. Much like her, he reflected grimly, either spitting disdain or melting in submission.

With a curse he put the car into gear and pulled away from the kerb with a rubber-burning squeal. The last thing he needed at this point was a redhead to distract him.

CHAPTER FIVE

THE HOTEL FOYER was also the dining room and actually the décor inside was much nicer than the façade suggested. About half the tables were occupied when Lara walked in, causing a few brows to rise. She walked straight over to Mark.

'I was worried.' He put down his newspaper.

It might have been more convincing without the petulant pout. *What did I ever see in him?*

'Really.' Her glance moved to the buffet breakfast he was tucking into. She struggled to imagine him spending his morning driving around the city to see that the woman he'd spent the night with was safe.

'As you see, I'm fine.' She spread her arms wide and hid her irrational hurt behind a flippant façade, trying to ignore the stares she was receiving from the other diners.

'So how do you feel about the Coliseum?' His glance slid down her dress. 'After you've changed, obviously.'

Lara shook her head and stared, not believing what she was hearing. 'What?'

'I worked out an itinerary. A weekend isn't long enough to see everything Rome has to offer, but—'

She moved closer to the table and lowered her voice to an incredulous whisper. 'You expect me to go sightseeing?'

'Look, this doesn't have to be a total disaster.'

His attitude made Lara want to hit his fat face. Actually, it wasn't fat. She held on to her temper with both hands and made herself look objectively at the man she had decided would be a safe bet.

Because that was what it boiled down to. In her determination to find a man who would see beyond her face and body she'd ignored other warning signs. One major flaw in her plan had been assuming a man capable of seeing her as more than a sex object would automatically be sensitive and caring, someone worthy of loving.

No one would have looked at Raoul and thought he was sensitive and caring, she mused, heat accompanying the image of the man she had spent the night with flashing into her head.

If she could have written a list of all the things

she had been consciously avoiding in a lover he would have ticked more boxes than she knew existed.

He was all the things, the breathing epitome, of what she had been avoiding in the man destined to be her first lover. Yet his raw, elemental sexuality had been matched by a gentleness and sensitivity... The only flickers of fear had been a fear of the strength of her own response, and that had quickly faded as she had embraced the passion that had blazed between them.

One of life's little jokes! It turned out she had wanted a man who would rip her clothes off and make her forget where she ended and he began.

With a sigh she tuned back into what a red-faced Mark was saying. 'The room is paid for.'

'Don't be ridiculous. I couldn't possibly stay here with you.'

Folding his napkin with irritating precision, he looked at her over the dark rim of his glasses and sounded annoyed as he asked, 'What's the alternative?'

Pushed into a corner, she bit her quivering lip. 'I want to go home.' She was embarrassed before she had closed her mouth over the unguarded words; his reaction turned her humiliation to anger.

'I thought I'd brought a woman away, not some little kid.' The defensive aggression that she had sensed beneath the surface was now overt as he added, 'I wasn't funding a school outing for virgins.'

'You weren't funding anything.' She had paid for her own flight. 'I'll leave the cash for my share of the hotel room on the dressing table before I leave.'

Turning, she stalked from the room and stomped her way up the stairs to the bedroom; not a room with a view—that was extra. Walking to the wardrobe, she pulled her clothes off the hangers and flung them in a heap on the bed before transferring them to her case. Next came the toiletries out of the bathroom. It might well be a record, she decided, turning the key on the padlock, for packing and stupidity.

She'd wanted to go away with safe and responsible and she'd got selfish and boring.

'You know, you're overreacting.'

She didn't bother to turn around but sighed and said in a flat little voice, 'Well, that's me, isn't it? A drama queen.'

'Not the best trait in a PA.'

He threw it in casually, didn't say outright that she'd be looking for another job as soon as she got home, but she'd need to have been stupid not to get the message. Lara's stomach went into a nosedive. So this was why office romances were frowned on. When they went sour bad things happened for the person who *wasn't* the nephew of the company owner.

'Don't worry. I've been thinking of moving on...' Her pride made her say it, but in reality she needed the pay cheque. Without it...she didn't want to go there! The only place she'd be going was back home with her tail between her legs.

Mark didn't immediately react. He crossed the room, picked up a tourist guide from the dressing table and shoved it into his pocket. When he finally looked at her she could see the relief on his face.

'That might be the best idea. Don't worry, I'll give you a good reference.'

She lost her struggle to hide her feelings. 'Don't make it sound like you're doing me a favour. I'm damned good at my job.'

'Yours, mine and everyone else's. Not everyone likes being told what to do by a secretary.'

Pride alone kept her chin up, *another* of her life choices coming back to bite her.

It was strange, but last night had not been a decision in her head, more a collision, one of those celestial events that nothing could stop…and if she could have, would she? The answer should have depressed her, but, in the face of Mark's unremitting nastiness, the fact it had happened made her feel not less in control, but more. She would never regret last night.

No, weirdly it had not been one of her bad life choices. University…? Lara had laughed at the idea—three years out of her life that gave her zero experience of *real* life and left her with a pile of debt hanging around her neck. Back then she'd had this crazy idea that talent and enthusiasm would make her rise through the ranks. Maybe true in some firms, but not in the one she worked for. Her glass ceiling had been set very low and her lack of paper qualifications meant she was never going to push through it.

There were no glittering prospects on the horizon, and until now she hadn't admitted it even to herself, because doing so would mean she'd have to admit she'd made the wrong decision.

'You know, sometimes it's better to admit you made a mistake,' she said.

'But if you fly back without me, people—'

She suddenly got it. 'You mean the guys in the office you told will think you're not up to it?'

'I didn't tell anyone,' he lied, red-faced. 'If *I'm* willing to make the best of this I don't see why you can't…'

Arms folded across her chest, she looked at him, not seeing sensitivity shining out from behind his horn-rimmed spectacles but a pretty boring, unimaginative and selfish guy.

'I'm really not your type, am I?' Part of his attraction, if she was honest—and that was long overdue—was the fact that Mark had never made a pass. She'd never had to fight off advances or ignore smutty innuendo.

It really ought to have occurred to her that he simply didn't find her attractive. She huffed out a laugh of self-mockery and thought, *That'll teach you, Lara, for assuming you're irresistible.* As for being the strong, quiet, heroic type—well, he hadn't even asked her where she'd been last night let alone made any attempt to find her.

Mark gave an uncomfortable shrug. 'You're beautiful, I was flattered, but—'

Suddenly Lara did not want to hear the *but*... which was not going to be ego enhancing. Hers had taken quite a battering, and if it hadn't been for last night and Raoul making her feel... She pushed away the thought. She was not going to turn into the sort of woman who needed a man to tell her she was beautiful in order to be comfortable in her own skin... *Skin!* A tingle slid through her body.

Images began to tumble through her head, relentless details, vignettes that had been indelibly imprinted. She could hear the soft rasp of her quickened breathing as she relived strong hands against her skin, gliding, and lips warm and moist.

It required every last ounce of self-control she had to banish them, to resist the compulsion to live it over and over. It left her feeling drained and strangely disconnected from reality, which might, she admitted, looking at Mark, not be such a bad thing.

His lips were tight—Lara recognised his fallback expression when Mark encountered any opposition.

'And anyway my CV could do with some polishing.'

Her comment succeeded in making Mark look uncomfortable; his eyes darted everywhere in the room except towards her face.

'I'll get the first flight home,' she informed him, and worry about how she was going to pay for it afterwards.

'You won't get a refund on your ticket.'

He was right, of course, she didn't, but the flight had not been as expensive as she had feared, even counting for the bus journey to the airport, which was miles out of the city.

Lara sat amidst frayed tempers and crying babies, sipping something that might have been coffee, when her flight was flashed up as delayed.

Just what she needed!

'Miss Gray?'

A tall man stood there, brown hair with some premature grey showing at the temples. He carried himself with an air of natural authority—of course, the captain's uniform helped.

She nodded, immediately wary; airports were not her favourite places.

'Is there a problem?' Her imagination went into overdrive, producing any number of disaster scenarios that would bring about this man knowing her name, seeking her out.

Did they send someone in a captain's uniform to inform you when your family home had burnt down or your mum was lying in hospital after a head-on collision with a bus?

He shook his head and flashed her a reassuring smile. 'Not at all. No problem, just a message.'

She touched a hand to her chest. 'For me?'

Her worried frown vanished as logic kicked in. There could be no message for her because nobody knew she was here. She hadn't explained her travel arrangements to Mark and nobody back home knew she was catching an early flight.

It was obviously a case of mistaken identity.

'I think you've got the wrong person.' And since when did men in pilots' uniforms act as messengers?

'No,' he said, looking at her hair. 'If you'd like to follow me...?'

When she thought about it later, Lara put her uncharacteristic docility down to a combination of the uniforms and airports, which were not the sort of places where anyone these days wanted to make a scene.

Airports! How she hated them! Though up to

this point the worst thing that had happened to her was lost luggage.

'I hope this won't take long, my flight—'

'Thanks, Justin, I owe you. Give my best to AJ.'

Raoul placed a hand on Lara's arm before leaning forward, hand extended to the other man. Lara stood there, too stunned to protest the possessive gesture as she watched the two men shake hands like old friends.

'Any time, Raoul.' *Justin* flashed a sheepish apologetic look towards Lara before setting his cap on his head and walking away.

It was a set-up.

As she turned her head to look at the man who remained the life returned to her stiff limbs. Snatching her arm free, she took an angry step away from him.

'Is he even a pilot?' she asked bitterly.

'Yes, he's a pilot. I called him when I got snarled in the traffic.' When Raoul had dropped her off and driven back to his place it hadn't been too bad, but by the time he'd reversed back out it had been straight into rush-hour traffic.

In the interim he'd not actually got out of the car.

The automatic gates closing behind him had seemed to act like a trigger. Without warning the dark thoughts that he had escaped for a few hours last night had come rushing into his head, carrying with them a sense of searing desolation and loss. Unable to fight the downward spiral, he'd sunk deeper and deeper, struggling like a drowning man. Just as his lungs had felt as though they would burst, he had caught a whiff of the perfume that lingered in the confined space, and he had focused on that elusive fragrance, letting it carry him clear.

Over in seconds, minutes or an hour, he had no idea as he sat there feeling as though he'd just run a hard set of sprints, sweat trickling down his back. He leaned back in the seat, pushing his head into the leather rest. The face that belonged to the scent materialised, and he let it form and solidify, allowing the image to push away the feelings of moments before. Sex had always been that for him, an escape, and now the echo of it was doing the same thing.

It was just a shame he hadn't realised sex had nothing to do with emotions before Lucy. Now he enjoyed it for what it was, which was a better stress-releaser than track work and as good as—though a lot more fun than—solo climbing.

Last night—even for someone who enjoyed sex as much as he did—had been...*incredible.* He focused on the lips of the face in his head and released a sigh of regret. If what she did for him came in legal prescription form, the next few months would be a hell of a lot easier to get through!

And then it hit him. Like a jigsaw the pieces suddenly slotted together, and he ignored the fact that some of the pieces needed forcing, and thought... *Why not?*

And then the rest just became clear. He would make the gloriously sexy Lara Gray realise that this was a business arrangement she could not turn down.

Even when she'd been sparking up at him with antagonism he could see that she had been as aware of the crackle of tension between them as he was, just less experienced at hiding the fact. She would come to see that *not* sleeping with her boss this weekend had been a great career move.

It was also his winning card.

The information he'd requested had come during the airport traffic jam. Owning a law firm with access to first-class investigators could be useful, and these days—as in post-Lucy—he backed up his hunches and gut instincts with hard, researched fact.

The file he'd scrolled through had been thin. It turned out that she didn't have a criminal record or any skeletons in her closet. She did have a driving licence and a couple of parking tickets, but no fall-back position if she lost her job, and pretty much no qualifications. Lara Gray needed a pay cheque, and her boss was the CEO's nephew.

Raoul was brought back to the present. 'Luckily your flight was delayed.' Raoul had had his jet put on standby to cover that eventuality.

He'd had no trouble rationalising what might on the surface *appear* an extreme course of action. He never committed to any course of action unless he was willing to follow it through; half-hearted measures were not his style.

Not that his *heart* had been involved, in this or any other decision he made. It was impossible to remove the risk factor completely, but it could always be minimised.

'Lucky!' Lara echoed bitterly as she continued to rub her arm where his hand had lain.

She couldn't brush away the invisible mark of contact any more than she could brush away the memory of the previous night. It seemed laughable now that she'd spent the bus journey to the airport convincing herself that in time the face that was etched so clearly in her mind would fade, the details would blur. There would come a time when she wouldn't remember his voice.

She had found the thought soothing because, though she wanted to remember her *first*, she also wanted to move past it and him. She knew how special last night had been and recognised the danger of souring future relationships by subjecting them to death by comparison. The idea of becoming the dating equivalent of a soccer-team star, who got to be thirty and still considered the winning goal he scored in high school the pinnacle of his life, filled her with horror.

And now he was standing there and the lie was cruelly exposed. Her protection was stripped away and the truth was looking at her through his eyes, his beautiful eyes.

Time was not a factor. His simply wasn't a face you forgot. Each angle and plane of his face, the subtle shading of his deep voice, the scent of his skin…it was imprinted, indelibly imprinted.

'Very few people can carry off the open-mouthed look.'

Lara closed her mouth with an audible snap.

'I didn't say you were not one of them.' To his mind Lara Gray could not look anything less than luscious if she spent a day trying.

'I don't understand what this little stunt is meant to achieve. Actually,' she said, lifting a hand to ward off any potential glib or even outrageous explanation, 'don't bother. I don't want to know. Maybe you've got nothing better to do with your time, but I have.'

'You're not even *slightly* curious to find out why I tracked you down?'

'No,' she lied.

His sardonic disbelieving smile made her grind her teeth.

'I don't want to talk to you.'

He shook his head in sympathy. 'I'd prefer to take you to bed too but—' He stopped, a rumble of laughter vibrating in his chest as he registered the blush on her face that continued to deepen. 'Let's go somewhere you can cool down.'

She ignored his hand and tucked her own firmly behind her back. 'I am not going anywhere with you. I have no idea what this is about, but my flight could be recalled at any moment and I need to be there.' She didn't have the money for another ticket.

'Relax, you'll hear from the bar when it's called.'

'But—'

'If you miss it I'll provide alternative transport.'

'Oh, really? I suppose you have your own private jet?'

'Yes.'

Her jeering mockery faded. 'I've no idea why you're acting like some weirdo stalker, but if you have actually got something to say to me you can say it here.'

'And have you pass out on me? You're pale as a ghost. Did you have lunch?'

'I don't pass out.'

'Or breakfast?'

Her stomach gave a loud rumble and, ignoring his grin, she muttered, 'All right, a coffee.'

Raoul led her to a table in a corner of the crowded bar-lounge, looking out of place among the groups of cheerful tourists. Without waiting for him to pull out her chair, she sat down.

Raoul shrugged, walked around to his side of

the table, and before he had taken his seat a waitress was there, eager to please.

'Coffee. *Grazie*... Lara?'

'Just a coffee for me.'

He responded in Italian this time and the girl bustled away after delivering a melting smile. 'I ordered you sandwiches.'

'Why did you ask if you were going to ignore me?'

A moment later, the waitress returned with their drinks and a plate of sandwiches, which she put in front of Lara, who picked one up. It would be churlish to waste good food just to prove a point.

She took a couple of bites; the slices of smoked salmon were interlaced with cucumber. 'So what is this about?'

'I have a proposition to put to you.' He saw her face and sketched a smile. 'Not *that* sort of proposition.'

Knowing her face was burning, she stirred her coffee and slung him a look of lofty disdain. 'I can't imagine I'd be interested in any sort of proposition you made.'

Unless it involved taking me to bed. She guiltily pushed the thought away and dug her even white teeth into the softness of her full upper lip, focusing on the pain, not on the ache low inside her.

'My grandfather is dying.'

Lara's eyes flew to his face. Her wary antagonism was crushed under a wave of inconvenient empathy. He looked as composed as he sounded, but she could intuitively sense the writhing emotions behind his mask.

She didn't know what she'd expected to hear but it hadn't been this. 'I'm sorry.'

His glance stilled on her face and she looked back at him through green eyes soft with sympathy. She hid behind a tough-cookie attitude and he could see why; it was inevitable that individuals who emoted that much frequently got taken advantage of.

Wasn't that what he was doing?

He shook off the moment of uncharacteristic doubt. He was not using emotional manipulation. This was a business deal, not a conventional one, admittedly, but he wasn't appealing to her soft heart, just her pragmatism.

'So am I.' He leaned back in his seat, his chest lifting as he exhaled and admitted, 'I've not really got used to the idea yet.'

'Has he been ill long?' she asked quietly. She'd

been a child when she'd lost her father but that had been sudden. Was it worse, she wondered, to know it was coming?

At least then you got the chance to say goodbye—something she'd always wished she'd been able to do.

'He's never been ill—at least, if he was I don't remember it.' His voice drifted away as he sat there seemingly lost in his own thoughts.

'Are you very close?'

He seemed to consider the question. 'He was more of a father to us than our father ever was.'

'So you have brothers and sisters…?' Maybe it was the lone-wolf thing he had going on that had made her assume he was an only child or even that he had emerged fully grown with designer stubble and a macho ego!

'I had a brother, Jamie.'

'Sorry,' she said again. His body language made it obvious that he wasn't comfortable with discussing personal matters, which begged the question, why was he? Raoul did not strike her as the sort of person who did anything without a reason.

'I'm not telling you this because I'm canvassing the sympathy vote. The fact that I'm the last Di

Vittorio standing is relevant.' Perhaps he ought to tell her that people around him had a tendency to drop like flies, but on balance he decided this might not be a vote winner.

He paused and appeared lost in thought again as Lara, curious despite her determination not to be, sat there willing him to continue.

'Family matters to my grandfather. He feels strongly about continuity, about living on in his children, passing on his genetic blueprint through the generations, a form of immortality, I suppose. When I was married he assumed that I would provide the next generation.'

'You're divorced?'

'My wife died. There were no children.'

His voice was a little dead as he gave her the information, just the bald facts that probably hid a world of pain.

'What is this about?'

'My grandfather's dying wish.'

'Which is…?' she prompted.

'To have his name live on in my child.'

It took her a few moments to digest his words. He couldn't be…no…she couldn't even think it, surely he couldn't, wouldn't? Outrage mingled with disbelief as she shook her head. Her chair scraped the floor noisily as she made an attempt to rise but her knees would not support her.

'Which is where you come in.'

A gurgling sound left her throat. He could not be suggesting… *Me!* She started to shake her head and, hands on the table edge, she pushed her chair back farther as if to physically distance herself from this insanity. 'You are insane,' she told him with utter conviction. 'And this conversation is over. I'm not going to be a baby incubator for you!'

'I wouldn't bring a child into the world just to please my grandfather.' When he had been considering his options that had never even figured.

She remained wary as she subsided in her seat. 'What was I meant to think? You said—'

'I want you to marry me, Lara, not have my children.'

'Oh, well, that's all right, then.' She lost the mocking smile, unable to decide if he was serious or this was some sick joke as she directed a searching look of pained incredulity at his face… Hell, he made it sound as though he'd just requested nothing more outrageous than directions! 'When my flight leaves I'll be on it. This conversation really is over now.' She jerked her hands to underline the finality of her statement.

His broad shoulders lifted, the shrug negligent, but the dark gaze that held hers was intense. 'Hear me out.'

She shook her head slowly from side to side. 'Nothing you can say will change my mind.'

'Then you have nothing to lose from listening to what I have to say. Give me the consideration you'd give any other job offer.'

She lifted threads of hair from her eyes, tucking them neatly behind her ears. Were you meant to humour insane people? 'Do you drink in the daytime too?'

He leaned in, the unexpected action bringing his face within an inch of hers. 'Smell?' he invited, parting his firm, sensual lips.

As his mint-scented, warm breath brushed her cheek, Lara jolted back in her seat so fast she almost fell off her chair. 'I'll pass, and, in case you forgot, I have a job.'

'*Not* sleeping with the boss is generally a good thing but in this instance…?' He shook his head and studied her face, letting the blush of discomfort develop before adding, 'I see you have worked that one out yourself. Did it not occur to

you to ask yourself if a weekend in Rome might
have consequences beyond losing your virginity?' Recognising it was irrational didn't stop
him feeling furious every time he thought of her
throwing herself away on some loser—any man
who let this woman walk away deserved the def-
inition. 'Do you *ever* think ahead? At what point
did it seem like a good idea?'

'How is your offer better?' she choked back,
eyeing him with dislike. Where did he get off
lecturing her?

His lips flattened into a hard line. 'Were you
hoping to hook him?' he speculated.

'Hook?' she echoed. *Does he think I need reminding of what an idiot I was?*

'Was marriage what you were after?' he cut
back, coldness seeping into his voice as other
features superimposed themselves over her vivid
face.

Lucy, his cold, calculating wife, had not done
anything as extreme as save herself for him. She
hadn't needed to… He felt a stab of familiar contemptuous self-disgust aimed more at his romantic, easily manipulated younger self than Lucy
and her mind games.

'If I was out to catch a rich husband—which,

by the way, went out with pearls and twinsets—I'd have chosen someone significantly richer than Mark.'

The furious flash of eyes like emeralds burnt away that other face and as she lifted her rounded, determined chin Raoul knew he had earned the dislike blazing in them.

Lara Gray was easy enough for a child to read! Not only could she not hide her feelings, she broadcast every emotion she felt on her beautiful face.

'It wasn't a judgement,' he said quietly.

She gave a snort. 'Not much!'

'If it's any comfort I think you got off pretty lightly. It can take some people a lot longer to realise the person they fell for doesn't really exist outside their own imagination.'

'Speaking from experience, are you?' she mocked, finding it totally impossible to imagine that situation.

He pushed his empty cup away from him, the action allowing him the time to smooth out his expression. 'Well, it wasn't all bad. Look, last night we had a good time.'

Lara struggled to fight her way out of the images that flickered relentlessly through her head.

He said, 'I made you forget.'

Where she began and he ended.

'And you returned the favour.' The dark glitter in his eyes was mesmerising.

The butterfly kicks had been a struggle to handle but now her stomach dissolved.

'So what do you think?'

She blinked like someone waking up and choked out, 'It was sex and it was one night.' She shook her head and loosed a shocked, incredulous laugh. 'What you're suggesting...beyond being certifiably insane—'

'Could work. I'm not asking for you to sign over your life.'

'Isn't that what marriage usually entails?'

'Have you read the divorce statistics? The contract I am suggesting would only last for...' he paused, the muscles around his jawline quivering before he voiced the grim reality '...my grandfather's lifetime, which according to the doctors is around six months, that or...' He stopped, cancelling the unnecessary codicil in his head: *until we want it to.*

He didn't like the vagueness of it, the sense that it was not within his control. No, there had to be a definite cut-off point.

His problem was thinking past the hunger she had shaken loose in him, a hunger he'd not felt, well, *ever*. Right now he felt as if he'd never be able to get enough of her. But inevitably he would; six weeks, six days…even this consuming passion had a sell-by date. It would not last as long as his grandfather, but, while it did, finding the sort of escape he had last night held a lot of appeal.

'He doesn't expect to see his grandchild, but being able to think there will be one will make his last days… It will give his life a purpose. Do you understand?'

Lara tried a change of tack, knowing that she was doomed to lose any argument that hinged on him *not* being the perfect lover and her *not* wanting more of what he'd shown her last night.

'I understand you're going to lie to your grandfather and you want me to help you.'

'You've never lied?'

She flung him a resentful glare. 'You know what I mean.'

'This is business. I'm not expecting six months of your life for free. You admit that you are going to be out of work…?'

She chewed on her lower lip. 'Probably,' she

admitted reluctantly. 'But that doesn't change anything.' *Except my bank balance*, she thought gloomily.

'You're right, there are always jobs for people with the right skill sets and qualifications,' he agreed blandly.

'I look on this as an opportunity to go back to school.'

'I like your glass-half-full attitude, but of course university fees are not cheap and you have to live, pay the bills…or you could give me the next six months and walk away with enough money to put yourself through college without going into debt.'

He mentioned a sum that would do a lot more than that.

'It would be wrong.' But it would really be a solution to the situation she found herself in…

'Why? Who would be harmed?'

'You're paying me for sex. That makes me feel like—'

'The sex is optional,' he said, hoping he would not live to regret the gesture, but as risks went it was barely registered.

Raoul knew about sexual chemistry but just breathing in the fragrance of her skin ignited a hunger in him that broke new ground. And he knew it was mutual. Lara Gray didn't have the ability to hide her own responses. And, yes, it *was* a massive turn-on to know that he could make her quiver without even touching her.

The idea that they could live as man and wife and keep sex out of the equation was the equivalent to throwing a lit match into a pile of dry leaves and expecting nothing to happen.

'If you chose to sleep in another bedroom, so be it.'

'And you'd be all right with that?'

His grin flashed at the note of pique in her voice. 'No, I wouldn't, but it wouldn't be a deal breaker.'

'I couldn't do it. I'd have to pretend that I'm… I'm…I'm—'

'Madly in love with me,' he inserted helpfully. 'That's precisely why it *will* work. You can't hide your feelings.'

'If you think that one night in your bed makes me in love with you you're seriously deluded!'

Her vehemence drew a dry smile from him. 'If I thought you were in love with me that *would* be a deal breaker. I have no need of love.' The contemptuous curl of distaste on his expressive lips backed up the claim. 'But love and lust can look very much the same to an observer. The sensual side of your nature has just woken up. I woke it up...you look at me and you want me—it shows.'

An embarrassed choking sound left her throat; he hadn't even attempted to lower his voice. 'You have a very high opinion of yourself,' she retorted, failing to come even halfway to delivering the haughtily contemptuous tone she was aiming for.

'So none of what I have just said is true?'

Lara shook her head. 'Look, I understand why you came up with this idea,' she babbled. 'I'm sympathetic, but if you just stop and think about it you'll realise it would never work. Your grandfather sounds like an intelligent man...?'

A smile quivered across his expressive lips. 'His brain makes razor blades seem blunt.'

She threw up her hands in an 'argument won' gesture.

He looked at her; the gleam in his heavily lidded eyes was sensual and teasing. 'He'll like you.'

'For my good child-bearing hips?'

Her stomach lurched as she watched the smile fade from his eyes, leaving something much harder and more predatory.

She knew that he was thinking of her naked… and she was thinking of him the same way.

'Will you stop doing that?' she pleaded. 'People might—'

Her agonised whisper made him grin, dissipating a little of the tension. 'People might, what, know your knees are shaking under the table and your throat is dry; they might notice that your pupils are so dilated there is only a thin ring of green left?'

The finger he placed to her lips silenced a fresh rush of denial, but not the voice in Raoul's own head that without warning acknowledged the fact he had so far successfully dodged: he *liked* Lara Gray.

CHAPTER SIX

LIKE. IT SOUNDED BLAND, not a dangerous emotion, but even so the discovery threw Raoul. He had female friends—he had never bought into the popular belief that men and women could not be friends. There were women he admired, women whose opinion he valued in and out of the workplace, but none of those women were the ones in his bed, because *liking* was not a prerequisite for good sex. Was it something he subconsciously avoided in sexual partners…?

With a slight shake of his head he dismissed the possibility and the significance of his discovery as he allowed his hand to fall away. She closed her eyes as his fingers trailed down her cheek.

It had been the lightest of touches, but the chain reaction it set up was not! By the time he took his hand away she was shaking and struggling to catch her breath.

She forced her eyelids apart and folded her fingers around her coffee cup to stop herself touching the side of her face where the skin still tingled.

'That is what I mean—you can't hide the way you feel, the way *I* make you feel. You've only just begun to discover your sensuality—'

Mortified beyond belief by his comments, she had really thought that she was being discreet. She said the first thing that came into her head just to shut him up. Just to stop him saying those things, which she could have dealt with if they hadn't been true.

It was just sex, you couldn't fall for someone you barely knew...just sex...just sex, she repeated in her head until the words became a meaningless hum.

'And I'm looking forward to continuing that process when I get back home with someone other than you.'

The words struck Raoul harder than a slap across the face. Without warning, images flashed across his retina, a stream of faceless lovers. Blood pounded in his ears as he fought to contain the outrage that threatened to spill out.

A couple of feet away Lara remained totally unaware of the effect her taunt had had on the recipient. It was the effect it had had on her that she was dealing with! The moment the words left her lips, the truth came crashing in—the thought of another man touching her as Raoul had made her feel… A shudder of revulsion rippled through her body.

'I don't want to have sex with anyone!' she cried out suddenly.

Her voice floated to him through a haze of anger. He shook his head to clear the low hum.

'Fine. As I've said that works too—you call the shots. I know marriage may seem extreme…hell, do you think I like the idea of going through with a farce? It feels like—'

'You're cheating on your wife?'

He gave an odd laugh. 'I certainly swore after Lucy died that I would never marry again.' His jaw clenched as he continued in a voice carefully devoid of emotion. 'But my grandfather means a great deal to me and if I can make him happy by disrupting my life for a few months it does not seem unreasonable.'

'He's not *my* grandfather.' It was ridiculous but she felt mean for pointing it out.

'Which is why I am offering an incentive.'

'You're trying to buy me.'

'Think of this as headhunting… You have a unique skill set that I want.' *I want you.*

'With sex as an optional extra?' she threw back bitterly.

'It would be a lie to say I am not eagerly anticipating sharing your bed,' he admitted, with a gleam in his eyes that sent a rush of receptive heat through her body. 'However, should the need arise the *palazzo* is a big place and you don't need to *see* me if you don't wish to.'

'*Palazzo?* I assumed we'd be living in your apartment…not that I'm going to be…living with… I'm not agreeing…'

He let her stumble on for a moment before permitting himself a smugly triumphant smile. 'See, a terrible liar.'

'For heaven's sake, being honest is not a defect, and I *can* lie.'

'I've never met anyone who wore her emotions so close to the surface.'

She lifted a hand to her temple, massaging the area to relieve a tension headache. 'No wonder I have a headache. You make me want to scream.'

'Now *that's* the truth, just as when you saw me you wanted to rip off my clothes…'

Before she could react to this casually voiced

and deadly accurate observation he cast a look of critical distaste around the crowded room. 'I think we should go somewhere less crowded…'

'I'm not going anywhere with you. I'm catching my flight,' Lara said, unable to shake the feeling she was fighting the inevitable.

'That might be hard—your flight was called some time ago,' he said gently.

'You heard and you didn't say anything.'

Raoul rose to his feet. 'We both know you're not going to fly out of here—you're coming home with me.'

The denial on her tongue died as he caught her eye.

Unable to maintain contact, she looked away, shaking her head. 'It wouldn't just be your grand-father we have to convince. What about my fam-ily? They'll think I've gone mad.'

'You can't tell them the truth, Lara. You can't tell anyone the truth.'

'Then what do you suggest I tell them?'

'That I am your soulmate.'

CHAPTER SEVEN

'OH, MY G—!'

Lara took her eyes off the tree-lined, private road they were driving along—it wasn't as if they were going to meet any oncoming traffic—to look at her twin sister's face. She imagined that she had worn a similar look a week earlier when Raoul had brought her for the first time to the family estate—her new home.

It was all deeply surreal.

'Yeah, it is a bit, isn't it?' It wasn't just the size and sense of history of the golden-stoned palatial house, but the magnificent setting. Cradled by a backdrop of mountains, olive groves covered the gently sloping hills to the west and a river wound its way like a silver ribbon to the north with the *palazzo* like a jewel in the centre.

'It looks like an illustration in a fairy tale, you know, not quite real, a bit like you getting married to someone you've only just met…?'

Lara focused on the road ahead, not reacting to

the unspoken question. 'Oh, there's Mum.' She nodded towards a plume of dust. 'We've almost caught them up.'

'It is incredibly beautiful, but don't *you* feel isolated here?'

The emphasis was not lost on Lara. She supposed it was her own fault. She had kind of played up how great the social side was when she had moved to the city for her job, but it was better than admitting that for the first six months she'd been terribly homesick.

'Without a night club within stumbling distance, you mean. I guess I'll just have to make my own entertainment, like in the olden days,' she mocked. 'I grew up in the country too, remember, only here there isn't a bus at the end of the lane, there's a helicopter.'

'And you have this.' Lily patted the deep leather upholstery of her seat.

Lara thought of all the cars in the garage that Raoul had given her the key code to on the first day, telling her she had her pick but warning her that the roads took some getting used to.

Up until now she had driven a 4x4 but this morning she had picked out the sleek sports car to pick up her mum and sister from the helicopter strip. Now she was regretting the impulse that might appear like showing off to Lily. In the end, when she'd arrived, Raoul's grandfather Sergio was already there with the limo.

'It is only good manners to meet your family,' he had reproached when Lara, already concerned that the hastily arranged marriage was going to exhaust him, had said he shouldn't have gone to so much trouble.

Her mother had been delighted to be driven to the house in the style to which she laughingly said she could easily become accustomed, but Lily had opted to go back with Lara.

Lara was glad it was a short drive. Lily had started in with the questions straight off, and Lara had avoided giving direct answers, then launched into a running commentary of the history of the house and estate. What she couldn't remember she made up, which, keeping in mind it was her inability to lie convincingly that had got her this gig, she felt she was doing rather well at.

If only Raoul were here to see her, she mused grimly, but he had flown off to Paris early that morning and wasn't expected back until tomorrow morning, barely an hour before the wedding.

He'd laughed when she'd accused him of avoiding her family but he hadn't denied it.

Wrapping a sheet around her, she had followed him out onto the balcony of their bedroom where he was taking his coffee. 'Even if Mum swallows this, Lily will know I'm lying. She'll definitely smell a rat. She knows even I wouldn't be insane enough to marry someone I've only just met.'

'Even I?'

'Lily is the sensible twin.'

He'd stood there with a look on his face that she had struggled to interpret. 'Sensible?'

'She wouldn't have agreed to this…and, no, you wouldn't have asked her.'

The odd look had come back, along with a smile. 'Then it is lucky for me I met the non-sensible twin. Relax, you do not have to prove anything to anyone, but if in trouble adopt the fall-back position.'

'What's the fall-back position?'

'Love is crazy, and we are deeply in love, *cara*.'

She'd tried to laugh but suddenly all she had wanted to do was cry.

She'd felt his eyes on her face as the silence had stretched. 'Try and relax. No one is going to question our motivation for getting married.

Why would they? I suppose a few might wonder if the haste means that you are already pregnant.'

The possibility had not occurred to Lara, who had reacted with a moan. 'Oh, no!'

He'd seemed bemused by her reaction. 'What's the problem?'

'You don't have a problem with people thinking I'm pregnant?'

'Fictional pregnancies I can deal with. Now, a real one...'

His expression had left no doubt as to what his reaction to *that* circumstance would be. Not that it was going to happen—he was meticulously careful in that way.

'I really don't think I can pull it off, Raoul.' She hadn't been able to keep the panic from her voice.

'Of course you can.'

The irritation in his voice had been reflected in his face as he'd lifted his eyes from the tablet his glance had drifted to.

'I wasn't expecting anything like this place.' She'd waved a hand to encompass the view, the room, and everything that went with it. 'I won't be able to keep up the act.'

'Nobody expects you to. It's not as if you're

going to be on show twenty-four-seven. You'll be living here. There are no cameras.'

'Oh, and there's nothing whatever daunting about that, and actually there are cameras.'

'Security cameras are there to protect you, not intrude.'

'Easy for you to say—you were brought up in a goldfish bowl.' She'd pressed a hand to her head and groaned out. 'This was a crazy idea.'

'Anyway, I doubt I'll be here more than one or two days a week.'

Her hand had fallen away.

'Did you think we were going to spend the next months joined at the hip?'

'Of course not!' she'd lied, trying hard not to examine the ambivalence of her reaction. 'Won't people think it odd…?' she had countered, keeping her voice light. 'Married couples usually—'

'Have a honeymoon, make babies…?' The mockery in his voice had morphed into a steely hardness as he'd spelt it out. 'This is not meant to be a real marriage.'

'How sweet of you to explain that to me.' Her glance had touched significantly on the sealed envelope that contained her copy of the prenup agreement that had been signed and witnessed the previous night.

He'd followed the direction of her gaze. 'You really should get a lawyer to look through those, you know.'

'I thought you were a lawyer.' Yet something else she hadn't known at the outset.

'I think they call it a conflict of interest.'

She'd shrugged. 'Why? Are you trying to cheat me?'

He hadn't smiled.

'Talking of cheating…if you want this to work it might be an idea if you're discreet…things like that might get back to your grandfather.'

'You are giving me permission to be unfaithful.'

Lara had felt her blush deepen under his sardonic stare. 'Oh, I know you don't need my permission.'

'You think after last night…' his dark glance had swivelled to the rumpled bed '…that I'd have the energy for other women? I will be *working* a twenty-hour day…jealousy is not part of your duties.'

Playing it again now, she could see how he had

misinterpreted her comments, but at the time she had been utterly taken by surprise.

'Jealous…! I am not jealous!' Then, in response to the voice in her head saying she was protesting too much, she had managed a less emotional, 'It's just the responsibility of your grandfather when you're not here falls on me.'

She had been massively relieved to see some of the suspicion clear from his eyes.

'You will always be able to contact me; if he needs me I will be here, and later, when his condition worsens, obviously I will travel less.' He had paused and delivered a hard, level look at her lightly flushed face that Lara knew she would never forget. 'Don't fall in love with me, *cara*.'

Even thinking about the warning made her skin burn with remembered embarrassment. Fall in love with him! She didn't even *like* him!

Lara shoved aside the memory of her response to Raoul, as beside her Lily continued to ask questions.

'So what sort of man is he?'

'He's the sort of man who would drag a woman off a flight to propose.' It was an inspired lie and, like all the best, had a basis in truth.

Lily's eyes widened. 'Seriously? He did that?'

Lara nodded.

'Wow, that is romantic.'

'Raoul is extremely romantic,' Lara lied cheerfully, before going on to invent several incredibly romantic gestures he had made. 'Here we are.' She released a sigh of relief as they drove through the last set of massive wrought-iron gates that closed silently behind them and pulled her car up beside the shiny limo that had preceded them. The massive main entrance door of the *palazzo* stood wide open, and presumably her mother and Sergio were already inside.

Lara got out of the car and waited for her twin, who came to stand beside her. The half an inch or so height advantage she had over her sister was cancelled out by the heels that Lily was wearing this morning.

Their tastes in fashion had always been different and today that difference was particularly apparent. Lily's floaty, flowered skirt fluttered around her calves, the top button of her simple sleeveless shirt was unfastened and her hair hung down her back in a shiny fat braid.

Lara wore a new acquisition, part of the wardrobe that Raoul had insisted she needed: a miniskirt in bold stripes of purple and lime green.

Her silk top was sleeveless too but was cut low enough to show the upper slopes of her breasts and glimpses of her lacy bra. Her flatties were soft turquoise leather ballet pumps and on the way out she'd slid a haphazard selection of bangles on her arm, which jingled as she pushed her loose hair from her face.

She watched her twin as Lily tilted her head back to take in the full impact of the building. 'I suppose anyone would want to live here.'

Lara's expression froze over. 'I hadn't seen the place when I agreed to marry Raoul and once you've met him you'll realise that his bank balance isn't the attraction.'

'I didn't mean…'

Lara ignored the horrified stuttered denial. 'There would be a queue around the corner for him if he only had the clothes he stands up in!'

Her sister touched her arm and handed her a tissue—Lara hadn't even known her eyes were leaking moisture… *What was that about?*

'I wasn't suggesting that you're a—'

'Gold-digger? No, really? Well, call me sensitive but…?' She had gone several steps before she took a deep breath and calmed down. Sensitive, yes. She recognised her reaction had been irrational but when hurt, her natural response was to hit out and she had. She wasn't even sure why the suggestion had hurt her so much.

'You love him very much, don't you?'

The soft suggestion made Lara spin around. 'I—' She stopped herself just in time from informing her twin that Raoul was exactly the sort of man she *never* wanted to fall in love with, and somehow managed a smile she hoped was sincere and maybe a little soppy.

'Yes, totally,' she lied, pitying the woman who fell for a man who seemed to be in love with a ghost.

One of her first conversations with Sergio had confirmed her earlier suspicions.

'I am so glad he has someone. After Lucy died he became…a shadow. Not all of him was here, the spark had gone, but you have brought it back for him.'

'I've never seen any photos of…her?'

With the aid of the cane he had taken to using he had got up, walked over to a bureau and opened a drawer. He had pulled out a gilt-framed photo and with a sigh of regret handed it to Lara.

'Raoul took all the photos down after she died, couldn't bear to see her face, I imagine. I don't know what he did with them but I kept this one. He doesn't know I have it.'

Lara had looked at the woman smiling out from the frame. The photo had been taken in the *palazzo*—she'd recognised the fresco from one of the first-floor salons. The way the light fell made it seem as though she were part of the Renaissance scene behind her, and there was a something of the angel about her, the silky golden blonde bob, the cupid's bow mouth painted red and her smooth, pink-tinged cheeks.

'She was beautiful.'

Evicting the angelic image from her head, she swallowed a slug of guilt when her twin hugged her.

'Then that's all that matters, isn't it? I just hope this guy is good enough for you, Lara.'

Her twin had made up her mind on that score before she even met Raoul.

'What,' Lily demanded as she paced the room, clutching her bouquet of wilting flowers in a white-knuckle death grip, 'could be more important than being on time for his own wedding?'

'He'll be here.'

It was weird, but the more tense and angry her

twin got, the calmer Lara became. Another time she might have appreciated the humour in the reversal of roles but not today. She was sure the stage nerves would kick in at some point, but not yet.

Maybe she wasn't nervous yet because it simply didn't seem real. The entire event had taken on the quality of a lavish film production. From the setting in the *palazzo*, a backdrop more glamorous and lavish than any film set, to the sharp-intake-of-breath guest list. It was an understatement to say that the Di Vittorios were well connected!

'Lily, dear, will you sit down?' Elizabeth Gray, looking too young to be anyone's mother, caught her daughter's arm just as the door opened to reveal the head of Security.

'*Buongiorno.*'

'He's arrived?'

'Signor Di Vittorio landed five minutes ago. He sends his apologies for any delay—apparently there was a bomb threat at the airport. Don't worry, it was just a hoax. He says the ceremony can begin when you are ready.'

'*Grazie*, Marco.'

'*Signorina.*'

'Is that man carrying a gun?' Lily asked when the door closed.

'Probably.' It wasn't until she saw her sister's expression that she realised how quickly the abnormal had become normal for her. What would normal life feel like when she returned to it? She closed off the thought, determined not to think that far ahead. She was committed now and there was no turning back. 'The security staff are not normally armed while Sergio is on the estate but with the guests here today...'

'Sergio apologised for it being a modest affair,' Elizabeth confided.

The twins both looked first at their mother and then each other before they all simultaneously burst into laughter.

The very *modest* affair was to begin with a service in the fifteenth-century chapel, while the wedding breakfast that followed was in the grand salon with priceless frescoes on the walls and views of the Tuscan hills. The doors had been flung open to allow the guests to mingle outside in the knot garden, where an orchestra entertained the guests.

'So that's it, then...' She gave her mum a tremulous smile and felt guilty when her mum's eyes filled with tears. Lara knew there would be another sort of tears six months down the line when the fairy tale ended.

'You look absolutely incredible, darling.'

Lara smiled and glanced down at the dress she wore, smoothing the ivory silk with her hand. 'It is beautiful.'

It was possibly the simplest of the creations that had been brought for her to choose between. Lara had expected there to be a few, but when she had walked into the room she had found racks and racks of amazing gowns, none bearing anything as tasteless as a price tag.

'No, my darling, *you're* beautiful.' Elizabeth pressed a hand to her trembling lips.

Lara smiled and thought of the face of an angel…an angel with blonde hair and red lips. Whose face would Raoul see when she walked towards him down the aisle: hers or his dead wife's? Did he close his eyes and think of Lucy when they made love?

The image in her own head leeched the colour from her cheeks until she stood there several shades paler than her dress.

She started as Lily leaned in and said softly,

'You can walk away now if you want to. It's not too late.'

Lara squeezed her hand, wishing she could tell her twin the truth. Would Lily understand? 'I'm fine, Lil.' Then turning to her mum, she held out her hand. 'Ready to give your daughter away? And with these around my neck...' she touched the string of matching antique emeralds that Sergio had presented her with '...nobody is going to be looking at me.'

And after the ceremony the emeralds would be safely back in the family vault along with the other Di Vittorio heirlooms.

It made her nervous to be walking around with the national budget of a small country around her neck, even for a short time. But there had been no question of throwing Sergio's gesture back in his face.

Infected by his mood, she had responded by asking him if he'd walk her up the aisle along with her mother. It wasn't until after he'd accepted with obvious delight that it had occurred to her it might not be the wisest idea. After a week here she knew that Sergio had good days when it was difficult to believe how ill he was, but he had bad days too.

The chapel was the opposite side of the *palazzo* from the suite of rooms where they had changed, separated by miles of marble-floored corridors, which today were lined with flowers and row after row of crystal vases, so many that the scent of orange blossom filled the air. She was aware of the occasional grim-looking suited figure as she walked along, smiling when she caught sight of one of the staff peering out from behind a door or around a corner to catch a glimpse of her.

Nothing about this could be less like the quiet wedding in a register office somewhere that she had imagined when she'd agreed to the plan. Not that it mattered really, the setting didn't alter the thing, and no amount of pragmatism could alter the fact that she was making sacred vows and she didn't mean a word.

Sergio stood waiting outside and smiled when he saw her.

'My grandson is a lucky man.'

Just when she thought she couldn't feel any *more* guilty.

'Thank you.' Lara laid her hand on the arm he held out just as the massive metal-banded doors swung open and a sea of faces appeared. Beside her she heard her twin gasp.

'It's Hollywood meets the United Nations! Oh, my God, is that…? Lara, there's *royalty* here…!'

'I know,' Lara gritted through a clenched smile.

Ironically it wasn't royalty that was bothering her—it was the less tangible presence of Raoul's first wife. How many of the people here today had watched when Raoul had exchanged vows with Lucy?

She gave herself a mental shake. It really didn't matter if there were people here comparing her unfavourably with the blonde angel—for some weird reason she couldn't see the woman's face without seeing a halo—what mattered was getting through this without being outed as a total fake.

The trick was just taking one step at a time.

As she began to move down the aisle, outwardly serene, inwardly she was panicking because two steps in it had become clear that this was *not* one of Sergio's good days. She could feel the tremors that moved through his body and the fingers that gripped her arm dug deep enough to make her bite her lip.

Now she wasn't worried about getting to the altar without falling flat on her face, she was worried Sergio wouldn't make the short distance without collapsing. She continued to smile, determined that the people watching would see her leaning on him and not the reverse.

Lara knew that for this proud old aristocrat to appear weak in front of these people would be devastating for him, and Raoul would blame her, and he'd be right to. She should never have made the offer.

Raoul stood there knowing before the organ burst into life that the reverent hush was for his bride.

It was a moment he had sworn would never happen again. The last time was enough for ten lifetimes and the poison it had left behind had burnt into his soul.

He took comfort in the fact that he would not fall in love this time—that this time his emotions were not involved. He'd fully expected to feel trapped at this juncture, he'd been *prepared* to feel it, but the emotion that separated itself out from the others was…actually, he couldn't name the feeling that tightened in his chest.

The circumstances ruled out pride, not that it was an unpleasant feeling to know you were the envy of every man in the room. She was beautiful. She was about to become his wife.

For six months anyway. The thought was chased

up by a vague sense of dissatisfaction, but before he could analyse it he realised that, though she was acting her head off, looking at him as though he were the man she wanted to spend the rest of her life with, all was not well with Lara.

For a split second he thought she was on the brink of doing a runner, then he realised what message her eyes were flashing as she turned her head slightly towards his grandfather.

Raoul stood ready to step in should he need to, right up to the point that Lara helped Sergio into his seat.

Lara felt as if she'd been holding her breath the entire length of the aisle. It wasn't until Sergio and her mother safely took their places in the front pew and she handed her bouquet to Lily that she could actually breathe properly.

She allowed herself a small congratulatory smile before she turned to face Raoul.

Their eyes connected and the lie hit her hard. The look in his eyes, the promises they were about to make. She felt the tears swim into her eyes and wished she'd opted for a veil.

The ceremony itself went by in a blur of emotion. She could remember Raoul's responses, his deep, clear voice, but not her own. Presumably she had made her vows because Raoul was bending his head for the first kiss, brushing his lips across hers and not acting surprised when she whispered the unromantic message against his mouth.

'It's your grandfather—I don't think he's well.'

His eyes held understanding but he just nodded as, hand in hand, they moved on to the legal part of signatures and witnesses.

At some point she saw Sergio leaving through a side door, his shrunken frame looking frail between two bodyguards.

She could feel Raoul's impatience as they stood welcoming their glittering guests, and by the time they reached the end of the line her hand was aching and she was way beyond awed and star-struck.

Once they were seated, Raoul got to his feet and the place fell silent, all eyes on the tall, commanding figure.

'I wish to thank all my friends and family for being here today, and most of all, naturally, my beautiful bride...' He paused for the ripple of applause. 'However, as you have probably already noticed, one person is not with us. Our host today, my grandfather, is feeling unwell, so

I will leave you for a moment in Lara's capable hands. Please enjoy yourselves.'

Lara watched him leave, noticing him pause to say something in the ear of a striking-looking brunette on the way out.

The woman nodded, then approached Lara with a friendly smile.

'Tell me, Lara, do you ride?'

She took a deep breath and thought, *And now I start earning my severance cheque.* 'I love horses, it's just heights I have a problem with. My sister and I did used to help out at stables near where we were brought up—the place is run by a charity that helps children with disabilities get an opportunity to ride.'

'I'm sorry.' It was close on nine when Raoul came to sit on the bed where Lara was wearing a pair of silky pale green shortie pyjamas.

She looked up when he spoke and shook her head. 'What for?'

'For walking out on the wedding reception...'

'How is he?'

She had got the message that Sergio's doctor had insisted that he go to the hospital to get checked over.

'They're keeping him overnight. They seem to think that there hasn't been any deterioration. It's his drug regime that's the problem.' He rotated his neck to ease the tension that had climbed into his shoulders.

Lara pulled herself up onto her knees and shuffled across the bed until she was in a position to slide her hands under the neck of his shirt. His muscles were like iron. 'Wow, you really have some knots there.'

Raoul grunted as her fingers dug into muscles. 'So how was it after I left?' He had felt guilty as hell leaving her to cope alone. Talk about throwing her in at the deep end!

'Oh, people were happy and there was plenty of booze. Actually, I left early myself.' Lily, who was at drama college, had a screen test for a TV show the next day, so she and her mum hadn't stayed late. Once they'd gone, Lara hadn't known a soul and Naomi, the woman Raoul had spoken to, who had introduced herself as a family friend, had assured her that she wouldn't be missed.

'Don't worry, I'll deputise,' she had promised as Lara had slipped away.

Raoul's silence made her wonder whether leav-

ing early wasn't a bigger thing than the other
woman had suggested.

'Did I do wrong? Naomi said she'd—'

'Oh, I'm sure it was fine.'

'Her husband is in a wheelchair?'

'She was one of Lucy's friends.' Actually the
only one he still had any contact with. 'And Leo
has MS. She's devoted and he's not an easy man.
Ouch!'

She dug her teeth into her bottom lip. 'Sorry,
got carried away,' she admitted guiltily.

He reached out and pushed his fingers into her
hair. 'You make it sound as though that is a bad
thing?'

His tone was light but the glow in his dark eyes
was anything but. 'You looked beautiful today.'
It was rare for his accent to surface; it only happened in moments of passion. 'I'm sorry the day
was ruined.'

'There's nothing to ruin. After all, it's all make-
believe, smoke and mirrors.'

'Well, you played your part well.'

'Did I? I don't really remember. I was just
scared that Sergio was going to collapse, and
this is all about Sergio.'

Recognising this didn't mean that she hadn't

wondered a little about how it might feel if this were happening for real...oh, not with Raoul, obviously. When and if she ever married again she knew it would not be a man like Raoul.

Even *without* the perfect-dead-wife thing there was the fact that he was the sort of man who could have any woman he wanted. She pushed away the thought—trusting him to say no was not her problem.

'Yes...but here, now, it is all about us...' His voice was a throaty caress as he leaned in until their lips were almost touching, then with slow deliberation skimmed his tongue across her mouth, tracing the full outline.

Lara was breathless, capable of nothing but gazing at him, the longing that infiltrated every cell of her body shining in her eyes.

'I'm going to be gone most of the week.'

She ignored the sinking feeling in the pit of her stomach. 'What will your grandfather think?' No honeymoon was one thing, but the groom leaving his bride alone the day after the wedding...?

'No problem, he understands.' He had understood better than Raoul the massive task it was going to be to bring his knowledge up to a level

where he could take the helm of the family businesses.

That makes one of us, Lara thought, stifling a
stab of irrational resentment.

'Oh, that's all right, then.'

Hard not to contrast her calm acceptance with
the reaction of a *real* wife. Right now he'd be
being made to feel as guilty as hell—a marriage
based on sex and a contract definitely had its
plus points.

'Feel like being carried away?'.

Lara curled her hand around his neck immediately, totally caught up again in the burning need
of the moment. 'Oh, yes, please.'

The next morning she woke at around six feeling groggy on the couple of hours' sleep she'd
snatched between lovemaking. The space beside
her in the bed was empty, but on the bedside
table stood a note, her name on it in bold, slant-
ing lettering.

Unfolding it, she read it.

*Meeting in Geneva at noon. Calling in on the
old man on the way. Any problems arise let
me know. If not should be back Fri p.m.*

It was signed with a flourish—but no *love*.

CHAPTER EIGHT

Three months later

LARA GAVE HERSELF over completely to the explosion of sensation as it hit, savouring the sweet release from devouring hunger.

Still breathing hard, she forced her lids apart as Raoul rolled off her and lay next to her.

'Oh, wow, that was—'

'Just sex.'

The words had pretty much the same effect as a bucket of cold water; they usually did.

She hid her hurt in sarcasm. 'And there was me thinking it was the start of something special, but I'm terribly grateful that you keep reminding me, because you're so irresistible I might not be able to stop myself falling in love with you.'

Raoul didn't react. He just levered himself out of bed in one fluid motion and began to collect the clothes he had dropped on the floor when he had not quite made it out of the door earlier.

'As you're a god among men…a—'

'Cut it out, Lara.'

She smiled and added sourly, 'Unfortunately no sense of humour, so that's it, I'm afraid. I'd never fall in love with a man who can't laugh at my jokes.' Or for that matter a man she knew every woman he encountered imagined naked. To marry that sort of man you'd need either impregnable self-confidence or a lack of imagination.

'I could never love a woman who—' He looked into the clear green eyes laughing up at him and his half-smile vanished.

There was nothing else to add. He *could* never love a woman. Love had almost destroyed him once; love was never going to enter into this or any other relationship he had.

He had been uneasy about the sense of connection he sometimes felt until he realised this was down to the fact that, since Lucy, his time with women had been counted in nights whereas he had been sharing a bed and his body with Lara for three months. Another three and she would vanish from his life.

Lara sensed his withdrawal. He did that so often—the sudden mood change, the broody silences—she'd stopped reacting to it.

'You've lost a button,' she said, watching him fasten his shirt and thinking he'd need a sense of humour or a stiff drink when she finally told him her news.

He dragged back his dark hair with an impatient hand. 'It doesn't matter. I'm late.'

She smiled. Late was good; late was a legitimate excuse for not telling him.

'So, Friday…?' She managed to say it as if not seeing him for four days were no big deal, but the truth was she missed him—or, as Raoul would have no doubt explained, she missed the sex.

The first twenty-four hours of their married life had pretty much set the pattern of the days and nights to come: he would leave on Sunday evening or Monday morning and come back Thursday or Friday.

Lara recognised she was pretty much the classic mistress, just with a ring and the social recognition that went with that. Social recognition meant she got treated with respect, which in turn meant she could have lunched out every day, had she chosen to, and was regularly asked to lend her name to any number of charities and good causes.

At first she had refused, until she'd realised she

was in danger of becoming the woman who only came to life when the man in her life deigned to share her bed. He shared nothing else though, which, as she frequently told herself when bitterness crept in, was a good thing.

She *couldn't* let herself develop any feelings for him beyond lust; she could not allow herself to feel things that would make her hurt when the arrangement reached its inevitable and sad conclusion.

She'd grown fond of Sergio, which was fine because she was *allowed* to be fond of him.

'No.'

Her eyes lifted to discover he was standing by the door. Lara shook her head. 'No?'

'I'm not going away this week.'

'Why not?'

His eyes slid from hers. 'I have a meeting with grandfather's oncologist later in the week.'

'Oh, right.'

'I should be h—back early.'

Now she was familiar with Raoul's work ethic and his relentless stamina, Lara was able to translate 'early' as somewhere between twelve and one a.m.

Too late to hit him with her bombshell.

Oh, she was delaying the inevitable, but why not? What was the hurry? Considering his attitude it was small wonder that she was dreading delivering the speech. She had tried a dozen versions, but nothing worked.

Maybe she should settle for a simple, 'I'm sorry,' because now it couldn't be just sex.

There was a baby.

After he left, she went back to the bathroom and pulled out the pregnancy-testing kit she'd hidden under some toiletries. She'd bought six and this was the last one left.

Her last hope.

Only there was no hope—she knew that even before she saw the line appear on the strip.

She spent the morning with Sergio. Roberto joined them mid-morning and they spent time going through albums, looking at snapshots of Raoul and Jamie when they were boys. In all the photos she had seen, Raoul's elder brother looked like a softer, fairer version of him—Raoul without the hard edges or dark outlook.

Though in the one that had got to her Raoul had had no edges. Nothing much more than a toddler, he had stood beside Jamie, staring not into the camera but up at his brother with an expression of childish adoration on his face.

The poignancy of it had filled her throat with tears that she couldn't hold back. It was her hormones, she knew that, but the two men with her had tactfully pretended not to notice her emotional reaction as she'd excused herself and left the room, leaning against a wall in the hallway before she gave in to the gulping sobs that shook her body.

By lunchtime she felt so tired she couldn't keep her eyes open so, after playing with the food laid out for her, she went to lie down.

She only intended to close her eyes but when she woke the clock told her she had slept for three hours. She'd missed her riding lesson.

She splashed some water on her face in the bathroom and, brushing back her hair, rubbed her pale cheeks to put some colour back into them before she went through to the bedroom.

Her heart stopped when she saw Raoul, who was hanging his jacket around the back of a chair. He looked up as she entered, his eyes darkening when he saw her.

'You're here…now… I thought…'

'I thought you'd be out…you look…' Raoul

reached out, clamped an arm around her ribs, and pulled her into his arms. His kiss was bruising and hungry, driving the breath from her lungs. 'Sorry about that, it's just I've been thinking about it all day.' He smoothed a copper strand from her cheek and kissed her again, more softly this time, his skilled lips gently moving across hers.

With a groan of reluctance he pushed her away from him and, heading towards the bathroom, growled, 'Hold that thought,' over his shoulder. 'I've been shut in an office with broken air conditioning trying to soothe senior management fears that I'm about to sack everyone just for the hell of it.'

Lara sat on the bed listening to the shower, wondering how he was going to react to the news. Not well was a given. Feeling dizzy with anxiety, she walked across to the chair and picked up his jacket, intending to hang it up properly. Raoul's phone slid onto the carpet and as she bent to pick it up she asked herself what she was scared of the most—becoming a mother or his reaction to the news he was to be a father.

For goodness' sake, Lara, just deal with it, because it really isn't going to go away.

A hint of defiance crept into her face as she looked at the phone, remembering all the times the shrill, teeth-clenching ringtone had proved there was always something more important than her in his life. With a determined little grimace she switched it off and guiltily slid it back into his pocket.

A moment later Raoul walked in, his dark hair slicked with water and his golden-toned skin gleaming like polished bronze against the dark towel he had looped low on his narrow hips.

Lara lurched from panic mode into weak-with-lust mode even before he reached her. The towel vanished as he laid her on the bed and slid a hand under her shirt over the warm skin of her narrow ribcage.

'I want to talk, Raoul.'

He stopped nuzzling her neck long enough to smile his brilliant head-spinning smile and ran his tongue across her lips. 'We can talk later.'

She had tried, she really had.

It was an hour later when she sat up in bed, pulling the sheet up to her chin.

'We really need to talk, Raoul.'

'I do not need to talk.'

She responded with a hissing sound of exasperation.

'Now?'

She closed her eyes so she could ignore the invitation in his eyes.

'Yes, now.'

'Fine. I'm listening.'

'Put on some clothes first.'

He looked bemused by the request and then smirked when she growled gruffly, 'I can't concentrate.'

'Right, will this do?'

She nodded. She had used the time while he dragged on a pair of jeans and a sweater to retrieve her skirt and shirt from the crumpled heap.

When the silence stretched he arched an interrogative brow.

Lara nodded and began to clear her throat but before she could launch into speech there was an imperative hammering at the door.

Frowning, Raoul opened it, barking out a question in Italian to the member of his grandfather's security team standing there.

The other man replied in the same language.

'My grandfather collapsed and was taken to

hospital two hours ago! Why,' he responded in icily articulated English, 'am I only hearing this now?'

'It's my fault.'

He swirled back to a miserable-looking Lara. 'What?'

'I turned off your phone,' she admitted.

'Why the hell did you do that?'

Lara shot a glance towards the staff member, who looked as uncomfortable as she felt. Raoul ignored the hint and raised a brow, intoning heavily, 'I'm waiting.'

Resenting the fact that he was treating her like a naughty schoolgirl, she couldn't deny how guilty she would feel if he didn't get to say goodbye to his grandfather.

'You looked so tired.' This was one of those times when even part of the truth sounded lame.

'I looked—!' He bit off his incredulous rejoinder and grabbed his key. He spoke to the solemn-faced messenger in Italian too rapid for Lara to even begin to follow and waited until the man had gone before he turned back to her. 'You're in danger of taking your wifely duties a little too seriously. You're here to look the part, not actually be it.'

She felt the heat of humiliation sting her cheeks. She'd crossed lines she hadn't known were there before, and made inevitable social faux pas, but previously he'd never lashed out at her for it. 'Fine. I'll move into the guest room, shall I?'

'That question might be academic.' He gave her one last furious look before leaving.

It was past nine when the phone finally rang. Lara picked it up, a feeling of sick dread in her stomach.

'He wants to see you.'

'How is he? Has he…? What's happened—?' She was talking to herself. Raoul had hung up.

Five minutes later she got into her car—well, the documents said it was hers, but, like her life at the moment, she knew she had it on loan.

Babies were not for three months or even six. Babies were for ever!

She pushed the thought away. She could barely deal with the present, let alone the unknown and scary future!

When she parked her car in the clinic car park, almost immediately one of Sergio's security detail appeared to escort her inside, and the man's normally impassive face showed signs of emotion as he told her that Sergio had been watching his favourite horse be put through his paces when he collapsed.

'Do you know how…?'

The man shook his head and stood to one side as she walked through the glass doors ahead of him. Raoul was waiting on the other side; the sight of his grey-tinged, exhausted face made her heart squeeze in her chest.

She was anticipating his anger; the relief that spread across his face felt like a kiss.

She caught his hand between both of hers. 'I'm sorry I turned your phone off. It was not my call to make. If I'd any idea…' she said earnestly. 'But I was with him this morning and he seemed to be having a good day.'

He shook his head, seemingly unable to take his eyes off his hand sandwiched between hers. 'I overreacted,' he admitted. 'He collapsed at the stables, and they airlifted him here. It's this way.'

Realising she was still holding his hand, she dropped it, muttering an awkward sorry before falling in step beside him.

At the door of the hospital room Raoul stopped and drew her to one side, aware as he did so of the scent of her hair. 'Just to warn you,' he began abruptly.

Her eyes lifted and his hands fell from her shoulders. He dug his hands into the pockets of his tailored trousers. 'He looks...'

With a soft curse he pulled his mobile from his pocket and turned away, but not before Lara had seen the blank screen or the expression on his face.

Overwhelmed by a rush of compassion that threatened to crush her chest, she could see the muscles along his strong jaw clenching as he outlined the situation. 'He's had a stroke, a complication of the drug regime. He looks...'

When his harsh voice broke, Lara's heart ached with sympathy. She touched his hand and he looked at her fingers on his wrist. For a moment she thought he'd shake her off but instead he turned his wrist and threaded his long fingers in hers, oblivious to the crushing pressure he was exerting. He took a deep breath and finished huskily, 'Broken, he looks broken.'

'I understand.'

Raoul doubted it. The doctor's warning had not prepared him for the reality of his grandfather's condition. 'Just don't let him—' He directed a warning look at her.

What did he think she was going to do, Lara wondered, look horrified or run from the room? *Is that the person he thinks I am?*

The answer was depressing. That was *exactly* the person he thought she was—a selfish, shallow thrill-seeker, an individual incapable of considering another person's feelings, let alone possessing any herself that might get bruised.

The knowledge hurt more than she was prepared to admit, even to herself.

'He's a proud man and for him this…' Bad enough that the cancer was eating him alive, fate had not even allowed him a dignified, clean exit.

Lara's anger subsided as quickly as it had emerged, replaced by guilt and a painful throb of empathy as she watched Raoul close his eyes, the muscles in his brown throat working as he fought to contain his own emotions.

'Of course,' she said quietly as she withdrew her hand from his.

Raoul preceded her into the room, his body initially blocking her view of the figure in the bed.

'Lara's here, late as usual.'

Despite Raoul's warning, Lara was shocked by the appearance of Sergio. Since she had known him, she had been conscious of the slow physical decline that even the best tailoring could not conceal, but the man in the bed attached to tubes and monitors, one side of his face twisted and frozen, was a grotesque caricature of the man who had once walked into a room and caused heads to turn.

Then she saw the eyes in the wrecked face. They were alert, so, squaring her shoulders, she donned a smile.

Raoul watched as Lara went forward, bending close to kiss the stiff cheek, something he had been unable to make himself do, before taking a chair and pulling it up beside the bed.

His grandfather spoke. The words perhaps had meaning in his head but they emerged slurred and garbled. Lara responded as though she understood what he was saying.

Raoul had no control over the emotion that broke free in his chest, and no cheque in the world, he decided, was big enough to repay the debt he owed her.

* * *

Half an hour later they walked side by side, not touching, to the car park.

'Are you all right to drive home alone?'

She turned her head but the glistening sheen of tears in her eyes made his face a blur. 'I could stay if you'd like?'

He stifled his instinctive response but the impulse disturbed him. There were times when he was aware that she gave more than he should expect and got very little in return. She played her part so well that often the 'supportive wife' act seemed real, not that he knew a lot about supportive wives, but he did know a lot about women who could act a part.

And that, after all, was what he had wanted. He had to remind himself that this was a job for Lara, not a life choice. And anyway, who in their right mind would choose to share their life with him?

Suddenly disgusted with his inability to face the truth and too tired to maintain the illusion, he accepted it. No relief came as he acknowledged that life with Lucy had broken him, he couldn't give or receive love, and that was a disability as much as a lost limb.

The knowledge lay like a stone where his heart once was as he shook his head.

'That isn't necessary. What did you say that made him look so happy?'

She lifted her eyes to his face, took a deep breath, and admitted with a rush, 'I told him I was pregnant.'

She watched as Raoul's dark winged brows lifted and a shocked grunt vibrated in his chest. A series of emotions flickered across his normally guarded features, finally settling into an expression of warm approval that lit a responsive glow inside her.

Lara had never needed anyone's approval in her life; even now with the glow inside her it was frightening to realise, to admit, how much she craved Raoul's good opinion.

'That was kind.'

She paused. This was the moment, but was it the *right* moment? Did the right moment even exist…? Then right or wrong it was gone, and the correction stayed in her head.

'Are you *sure* you're all right to drive back alone?' he asked again, noticing for the first time the pallor of her creamy skin and the faint shadows beneath her emerald eyes.

Had she lost weight recently? he wondered, his suspicions aroused as he took in the prominence of her delicate collarbones.

'You're not on some stupid diet, are you?'

Lara responded to his glowering disapproval with an odd little laugh and moved her head in a negative motion.

'I'm fine.' Pregnancy was not a disease, though she suspected the person who had said that had never suffered from morning sickness.

He made no comment but didn't look entirely convinced as he pulled his eyes from the visible blue-veined pulse that beat at the base of her throat and directed a hard look at her face.

'I thought I'd stay a while, sit with him.' His dark eyes shifted to the low sprawling terracotta-tiled building behind them that looked more like a hotel resort than a private hospital. The one thing his grandfather had not wanted was to spend his last days in a hospital bed. But life was filled with things that a man wanted but could not have, he thought bleakly.

'Let me stay, Raoul…?'

He shrugged. 'What would be the point?'

She hid her hurt at the rejection under a smile

and withdrew the hand she had extended towards him. 'No point at all.'

The phone call she had been half expecting came just after midnight. Lara was sitting on the balcony of their bedroom breathing in the fragrance of the pines on the warm night breeze. It was the call she had been expecting, but not the caller.

'Hello, Lara, I hope I didn't disturb you.'

An image of the elegant, petite Italian brunette flashed into her head.

'Not at all, Naomi,' she said, wincing at the stiff formality of her response and wondering why she could never relax around the Italian woman.

'Raoul asked me to ring you and let you know that Sergio passed away about an hour ago.'

Lara's sadness was alleviated by the knowledge that the proud old man would not have to suffer any longer. 'Thank you for letting me know. Raoul, is he at the hospital still? I'll come—'

'That's fine, Lara, he asked me to tell you not to come. Don't worry, I'll look after him.'

It was around three in the morning when Raoul arrived back at the *palazzo*. Lara heard him and called out from the library where she'd been awaiting his return.

'I thought you might come.' He struggled to keep the note of irrational accusation out of his voice. Naomi had relayed Lara's message that she wouldn't be coming.

'I don't blame Lara one bit. Who wouldn't want to stay in their warm bed? The last section of that road would be any tourist's nightmare, Raoul.'

He felt a stab of guilt. Naomi had been really supportive and his response to her comment had been a lot sharper than he'd intended.

'Lara isn't a tourist, she's my wife.'

But for how much longer?

Finally acknowledged, the question refused to go back to the dark corner he had consigned it to. Such avoidance was not like him. Raoul could only suppose that his behaviour had been influenced by his grandfather's determination not to live his last days in fear of the future but instead extracting every last ounce of pleasure from the time he had left.

Not that the future involved any fear for Raoul, not even any major inconvenience. He had left nothing to chance; the arrangements were in place to painlessly dissolve this marriage when it had served its purpose.

Admittedly, knowing that *the moment* was passing made him realise just how much pleasure it had held. And though he had refused to acknowledge how risky this strategy was, he admitted now that this could have turned out very badly indeed. Marrying Lara to make his grandfather's last days happy could have been a major crash and burn.

But though living with a woman who threw herself at everything, be it a pasta dish, a walk on a beach or sex with uninhibited enthusiasm, might be at times exasperating, it was also exciting. She perfectly encapsulated living in the moment.

Thinking about a future minus that excitement deepened the furrow between his strongly delineated brows but a woman like Lara demanded more time than a man like him could offer.

Couldn't, wouldn't, won't...?

His comment and his accusing attitude bewildered Lara. 'Naomi said you didn't want me to.'

The furrow between his dark brows deepened even more; she had obviously misunderstood. 'I took her home.'

Of course you did, she thought, standing motionless as the sick, angry jealousy grabbed her in a chokehold. 'How come she was at the clinic?'

'Her husband is there having some treatment.'

The explanation immediately made Lara feel ashamed of her gut response; the woman had never been anything but kind to her and if Raoul had friendships with other women it was not her business. If it was more than friendship? It still wasn't really her business.

'You look tired.'

He shrugged and walked across to the bureau. She watched as he poured brandy into the bottom of a heavy tumbler and raised it to his lips. 'To you, you old bastard.'

Her nostrils twitched as the aroma produced a wave of acid nausea in her stomach. 'It might help to talk.'

Catching her worried gaze, he emptied the glass in one swallow. 'I don't want to talk.' He dragged a hand through his dark hair. 'I don't want to think… I just want—' He reached out towards her, his eyes burning with unvarnished need.

Then before she could react his hand fell. A spasm of self-loathing contorted his dark features as he slammed the glass down. He was using her and acting as if it were all right.

'I'll sleep in the study tonight.'

Lara was utterly confused by his mixed signals but also by the morass of conflicting emotions. She put it down to crazy hormonal changes and cried herself to sleep in the bedroom alone.

CHAPTER NINE

How was Raoul?

'I don't know,' Lara admitted. 'It wasn't really unexpected, but no one expected it to happen so soon. Raoul has been busy with arrangements… with the funeral.' The event, which was being attended by more than one state leader, required a lot of planning, yet another excuse for her to delay telling him about the pregnancy. And anyway it seemed to Lara that he was avoiding her.

Maybe as far as he was concerned the contract between them was already over?

'Ring me tomorrow when it's over…?'

It's already over! 'Sure,' she managed dully, suddenly feeling more alone than ever before.

'Look, you know I'd really like to come, to support you if I could, and so would Mum…'

Lara closed her eyes and fought back tears. 'It's fine.'

'It's not. It's just that I have a hospital appointment tomorrow and Mum is coming with me.'

Lara's stomach muscles tightened. 'You're ill?'

'No, the thing is, I'm pregnant.'

'Pregnant!'

'Yep, and at the moment I'm as sick as hell.'

Tell me about it!

Lara just stopped herself, biting her tongue hard enough to make her wince. It was so tempting to offload, to share something she had in common with her twin, but she couldn't tell Lily before she told Raoul. She would tell him...when the right time came.

'I thought it was supposed to end after three months.'

The implication of the comment hit Lara. 'Three months...so how far along are you?'

'Twenty weeks...it's not just you I haven't told, Lara. I've not told anyone. I think I was pretty much in denial, but now I've kind of exploded overnight.'

Lara barely registered the forced humour in her sister's voice. 'You're *five* months pregnant.' She pressed a hand over her own still-flat stomach. 'You were pregnant at the wedding?' There had never been any psychic connection but shouldn't she have sensed it? How could she have, when she'd been too busy keeping her own secrets to guess her twin might also have something to hide?

'It was *your* day, Lara.'

My day... She stared at her hands, feeling the tears that flowed too easily well hotly beneath her eyelids. She blinked them back and focused on the gold band that encircled her finger, suddenly aware her sister had been talking and she didn't have a clue what she'd said.

She lifted the gold band to her lips, remembering him sliding it on and how *right* it had felt. Without warning, the protective shield she had been hiding behind slid away, revealing a truth she could no longer run away from. She was staring at the truth…the glaringly obvious truth.

She'd told herself she was acting, that it wasn't real, but it *was* real. She was in love with Raoul—he had warned her not to but she had anyway.

He was *everything* she'd been determined to avoid in a man and yet he was everything she needed, she craved… She closed her eyes, wishing herself back to a time when she had imagined you could control who you fell in love with, that you could choose *safe* love, when in reality you had no more control over love than the colour of your eyes.

The level of her blind stupidity seemed incredible. Love had nothing to do with self-control or common sense; she had no choice whether to love Raoul and it didn't matter if he wanted that love, if he rejected it *and* her.

She loved him with a soul-deep passion and would carry on loving him even after he broke her heart.

The rest of the phone conversation was stilted and awkward but Lara barely noticed. It wasn't until she put the phone down with a shaking hand that Lara realised she hadn't even asked her twin who the father of her baby was!

The day of the funeral was warm, thunder rumbled in the distance but the rain waited until after Sergio had been laid to rest in the family vault.

The afternoon sun hit the study at the *palazzo*, and it was still uncomfortably warm as Raoul entered, putting his glass on the desk littered untidily with papers. He pulled open the French doors and stood there, eyes closed, breathing in the cool evening air before taking a seat in the padded leather chair beside the desk.

The mourners who had come back to the house after the service were gone...and so was his grandfather. His eyes went to the open door. Even now, he half expected to see the old man framed in the doorway.

But he wasn't.

Raoul had stood up and told the mourners that for Sergio Di Vittorio family came first.

He could with equal honesty have added that the old fox had also been a master manipulator who could be utterly ruthless when it came to getting his own way.

He had died thinking he had got his way one final time, Raoul thought as he lifted his glass in a silent salute.

The twisted smile on his face vanished as he put down the glass, his thoughts sliding back to earlier when she had told him that they needed to talk. It was obvious what that would be about.

Her future, the one she would have without him. It would be a good one. She had talent, though he doubted she recognised yet how much. She deserved good things, he told himself, ignoring the sinking feeling inside. If he analysed it he'd have to admit that he wanted her to stay— not for ever, obviously, because there was no for ever, but just for a while, just so that he could carry on enjoying her.

When he'd met Lara his life had been disintegrating around him. He had lost or been losing everyone he'd ever cared for, but she had kept him afloat. Of course, having her around was going to make the next few weeks easier, but after that what…?

After that, nothing, because Raoul knew he had nothing to give. He was disgusted with himself for it, but he knew that what he was good at was taking. He knew it would be easy to persuade Lara to stay longer; he knew he was good at manipulating her feelings. But for once he was not going to put his own selfish needs first.

And then he could get back to life as usual.

I thought you'd fallen off the planet, darling!

At first he hadn't even recognised the woman who had virtually collided with him in the street. Her name had continued to elude him as she'd pressed a kiss to his mouth. Just in time to save embarrassment it had come to him, along with the location of their fling a year or so ago.

She'd looked at his wedding ring and aimed a speculative look at his face. 'Married, but how married?'

He'd made an excuse and left without respond-

ing to the question or the unspoken invitation in
her carefully made-up eyes.

That was *his* life, the one he had chosen, the
one he would go back to, just as soon as he was
done with Lara.

Refusing to acknowledge the feeling that gath-
ered strength inside him until it came perilously
close to icy panic, he clenched his jaw and slowly
rebuilt the barriers he had put up in order to survive his first marriage.

He was better off alone.

Not yet though; for the moment Lara was still
here.

Was she still asleep? It had been three when
she had finally confessed to not feeling well and
then only after a lot of prompting.

Naomi had offered to help her to her bedroom
and Raoul had looked in on her later, after the
last of the mourners was gone. She had been fast
asleep.

A sound made him turn his head. Framed in
the doorway where he had just imagined his
grandfather was Lara, her hair long and loose,
glowing against the black fabric of the simple
shift dress she still wore. She didn't move as
their eyes connected.

'Are you feeling better?' he asked, refusing to acknowledge the tightening in his chest as anything other than a natural protectiveness. She nodded and walked into the study, her bare feet silent on the wood. Her eyes looked enormous in her pale face and the milky pallor of her smooth skin emphasised the delicate purity of her cleanly drawn features.

'I'm fine,' she lied, struggling to throw off the lethargy that seemed to weigh down her limbs. 'I slept.'

She had fallen into a deep sleep only to wake and find Naomi standing beside her bed, causing her to let out a startled squeal of alarm.

'Sorry, I didn't mean to wake you, but Raoul was worried and he asked me to look in.'

If Raoul was so worried why couldn't he look in himself? Even acknowledging the thought made her feel guilty; Raoul had buried his grandfather today and she was acting like an attention-seeking brat.

'Thank you, I'm fine.'

To her dismay the other woman sat down. 'I hope you don't mind,' she began hesitantly, 'but I've noticed... Well, I've got the impression,' she corrected, 'that you feel you're living in Lucy's shadow.'

Lara was simply too astonished to respond.

'You have nothing to live up to. Lucy was a bitch,' she said simply.

Lara thought she had misheard. 'Pardon? I thought—'

'She was a bitch.'

'I thought she was your friend?'

'She didn't have friends, just people she used. She made Raoul's life a misery, and she knew all along that he loved someone else, but they cannot be together. I am so happy to see that Raoul has someone to make him happy now. I'll let you rest.'

Lara watched her go, not knowing what to make of the one-sided conversation. It wasn't just *what* she had said, it was the way she had said it…the secret little smile… She shivered, very much unsettled by the woman's manner.

Naomi hadn't actually meant that *she* was the person Raoul couldn't be with…*had she*? Lara thought about all the occasions she had seen them together or at least in the same room. There would have been signs, she'd have picked up the signals, wouldn't she…?

On the other hand, she had managed not to know she was in love with him for months. Maybe signals weren't her thing. Did any of this even matter? She'd be out of his life soon…except that there would always be the baby… Would he even want to be part of the baby's life?

Just what she needed—another unanswered question to add to all the others!

With a deep sigh she sat up and propped a pillow behind her head, running over Naomi's words in her head again and again. The more she thought about it, the more it felt *off* somehow. As was the idea that Raoul's marriage had not been happy, that his perfect wife had not been quite so, well, perfect.

It seemed much more likely that Naomi had a thing for Raoul and was making up stories about a poor woman who couldn't defend herself. The only way she'd know for sure was to ask him.

'Now there's a revolutionary thought, Lara,' she whispered mockingly to herself, and made her way downstairs to find Raoul.

'Sorry I skipped out like that.'

He shrugged, dismissing her apology as he dragged a hand across the dark stubble that al-

ready dusted his jaw and lean cheeks. He closed
the laptop that had been sitting open on the desk.
It was all for show—he hadn't been able to focus
on work or even read his emails or any of the
messages of condolence.

'I coped.'

'It's been a hard day for you.' Her heart ached
for him; he looked so tired, so sad.

After a pause he acknowledged this with a tiny
tip of his dark head, while privately acknowledging the fact that she had made it easier. Her quiet
presence beside him, support expressed with a
touch and a look.

'I should have been there.'

'Naomi was only too happy to stand in.'

He felt ungrateful but he'd found it impossible
not to compare Naomi's practised social skills
with Lara's more instinctive ones… Oh, there
was no doubt that the woman could work a room
and she never said the wrong thing, but then her
smile was never genuine either and her laugh
never uninhibited or too loud.

Not that there had been much to laugh about
today, he thought sombrely, but Lara had not just
given the impression of listening to the long-
winded reminiscences of the elderly friends of

his grandfather's, she *had* listened. It didn't matter who had been talking; he was pretty sure that mostly she didn't have a clue who they were— or how important. At one point he had seen her spontaneously grab his godfather and hug the man!

Just after Lara had slipped away the elderly but still-influential Greek shipping magnate had taken Raoul to one side and shaken his hand, telling him that he was lucky indeed in his wife: *'A keeper, my boy, but if I was thirty years younger you'd need to watch your back!'* he'd chortled.

For a man who would have preferred to walk in front of a bus than get married again, this arrangement with Lara was actually suiting him. Plus, the sex was incredible.

He wished they could extend the arrangement, but he had come to see the real Lara, to know her, and she deserved more...

Lara deserved better than him.

Closing the open French doors on a breeze that had sprung up, he missed Lara's flinch at the mention of the other woman's name.

'Has she gone?'

'Who?'

'Naomi.'

He nodded, making a mental note to have a tactful word—she had been dropping around a little too much lately.

'You should have stayed in bed.'

'Were you happy?'

There was a hushed, husky vehemence in the abrupt question that made him look at her sharply, sensing suppressed emotions that showed their physical presence in the restless twisting of her long fingers. Something was going on in that beautiful head and he didn't have a clue what it was. He allowed frustration to mask the protectiveness that made him want to take her in his arms.

'Was I happy when?'

'People say that you had a perfect marriage.'

'Do they?'

'Did you love her…your wife? Were you happy?'

In a voice edged with steel he cut across her. 'You're my wife.' The word had always carried with it negative connotations…yet there had been times when he had said it recently when he had felt…*proud*…?

The interruption didn't stop her; she'd gone too far and she *had* to know. 'You know what I mean.'

He turned his head and directed a flat stare at her face. 'No.'

'I was asking—'

'I know what you were asking.' He gave a twisted smile. 'I was answering. No, I was not happy, well, for about five minutes, but once I woke up, or grew up, or both, I was not.'

'If you were unhappy why didn't you just get a divorce?' *And marry the woman you apparently love so much but can't have?*

His mouth twisted into a parody of a smile as he turned to face her, dragging off the tie that was still looped around his neck as he did so. 'In a perfect world I would have, but the world…' he let the tie slip through his fingers and fall to the floor '…and life,' he continued harshly, 'are not.'

'I don't understand.'

'Of course you don't.'

How could she? There were no dark depths to Lara—she was the diametric opposite to Lucy, who on the surface had seemed so wholesome and sweet but the moment she was crossed revealed herself to be spiteful and vindictive, a person who thought the world revolved around her.

'Then explain.'

Well, he certainly hadn't learnt from his mistakes with Lucy—he had taken Lara at face value, and ignored the sweet, vulnerable angel beneath the beautiful but hard shell.

He'd clung stubbornly to the image, but each day together had eaten away at it until he couldn't pretend any more.

Understand... How could she? Lara had a conscience and empathy; she had no desire to see those who thwarted her suffer; she didn't need a constant, exhausting supply of attention and admiration or react with vicious spite when she didn't receive the praise she felt she was entitled to.

'Please, Raoul, I want to understand.'

The court-enforced appointments with the therapist following the hushed-up 'incident' that had left Lucy's hairdresser with a black eye had been illuminating but not in themselves helpful.

At the end he'd known all about borderline personality disorders and malignant narcissists, but as Lucy had refused to accept she had a problem it had meant little in reality.

'When I was married Jamie was never officially out. When he was still a student Jamie fell for a man who was…in a position of power, a married man, and they had a long-term affair. If the truth had emerged this man's career, his marriage, his life would have been over. One night Jamie started to talk. We'd been to dinner, had a few drinks... Lucy was very sympathetic.

'So when I told her that it was over she told me that if I filed for divorce she would out Jamie and his lover, that she would give interviews to every scandal sheet and tabloid she could find.'

Lara was appalled. She simply couldn't get her head around anyone who wanted to hurt other people. 'Your brother...'

'Didn't know.' He rubbed a hand across his forehead. 'The irony was, a month after she was killed in the crash he and his lover broke up; the next month he met Roberto.

'Lucy was the heroine in her own life story. Every story heroine needs a villain and for her that was me. To understand Lucy you have to realise that she did not just need to win, she needed to take everything away from everyone else, turn their friends against them, strip them of pride; her lust for revenge was utterly insatiable.'

Lara shook her head, finding it impossible to reconcile the angelic image in her head with the...*evil* he spoke of.

'The deal,' he explained in the same flat voice, 'was that we stay together…the public act was part of her punishment; she liked to see me help-less. She enjoyed flaunting her affairs, telling me she had aborted my child…laughing…'

Lara had sat dry-eyed and composed through the remembrance service; even when Raoul had paid his moving tribute to his grandfather she had kept the tears at bay. But now they flowed. 'Oh, God!' she sobbed. 'How could she, how could anyone…be so…? A baby…'

'She sent me a scan photo for my birthday, in-side a daddy card.'

Lara pressed a hand to her mouth to hold the cry of horror inside. Like everyone else, she had looked at Raoul and seen the aura of power that he wore like a second skin, the cynicism, the edge of ruthless determination.

Now she saw the idealistic young man he had been before his first wife, the man he had been before he had been subjected to emotional tor-ture by the person he had thought he loved. Her heart ached for him, the man he was and the man he could have been, had the evil woman not torn away his belief in goodness and love.

Would he ever heal?

Raoul felt an unfamiliar helplessness as he watched the silent tears fall down her face.

'It is in the past and gone,' he said abruptly. 'I am the man I am now, and it's better that I stay alone. I know not every woman is like Lucy, but I can't trust anyone, and even if I could I have nothing to give that sort of woman, not the things she needs.' His dark eyes held hers for a long moment. 'Do you understand what I'm saying, Lara?'

'You want to be alone. Doesn't that mean she has won?' He said nothing and she gave an angry sniff, choking out another gruff, 'I'm sorry,' while wiping away the moisture from her face with the back of both hands. 'I would like to tear her hair out… She's dead, that probably sounds terrible, but I don't care!' she cried.

'I know terrible, and, trust me, that is not.' He studied her pale face. 'You look like you could do with a drink,' he said, losing the battle to hide his concern.

'You should have told me.'

'Why? You think I want to advertise the fact I was a fool? I've never told anyone before—the whole world but you swallows the party line.'

The contempt in his voice made her wince. It

was clearly aimed at himself. She didn't say anything because there was nothing she could say. Instead, she watched him pour brandy, wondering how she could refuse without it seeming odd.

'No, thanks, I won't. Actually I think Naomi knows.'

'Naomi?' He thought about it and nodded. 'I suppose she might know some—she and Lucy were close at one time, though I think she dropped her before the end,' he recalled with an uninterested shrug. 'And Lucy liked to boast about her triumphs.'

'I know now is not the right time, but I really don't think there's ever going to be a good time.'

'You want to make arrangements to leave.' Eyes dark and bleak turned her way but his shrug was casual. 'There's no hurry.'

'Good, no, I mean…' She took a deep breath and thought, *It's now or never.* 'That is not what I wanted to say. I've been trying to speak to you for a while… You see… Actually there's a…complication.' She swallowed. 'Oh, Raoul,' she husked out. 'I'm so sorry.'

His jaw clenched. 'Will you stop saying sorry?'

'Sorry.' She bit her lip to stop another sorry falling out. At least *sorry* was better than *I've fallen in love with you.* The words were so clear that for a moment she thought she'd spoken them out loud.

He arched a brow.

'I didn't lie to your grandfather.'

Comprehension spread across his face—how like the Lara he had come to know to get hung up over a lie. 'You lied for the right reasons.' He reached for her hand but she didn't take it; instead she brushed a few fiery, silken strands of hair from her brow.

'Our marriage was a lie.' On more levels than he knew.

Her use of the past tense deepened the frowning line between his dark brows.

'At times a lie is the kindest thing.'

'Not a kindness. You see, I *am* pregnant—not pretend, for real.'

The delivery was everything she had intended, measured, calm, but then she spoilt it all by bursting without warning into tears, loud sobs that seemed to be dragged from somewhere inside her. 'I'm s-sorry!' she managed between choking gasps.

Raoul didn't move; he just stood there with the

look of a man who could see a ten-ton truck approaching and couldn't get out of the way.

Lara's knees folded and she sank down into the nearest chair. 'A shock, I know, and I'm sorry, but when you've had time to take it on you'll realise as I have that it doesn't have to change anything.' *He still didn't love her.*

Raoul, who had been standing silent, surged into motion, dropping down on his knees beside her chair.

'It changes *everything.*' He knew this, though the details of these changes remained beyond him at that moment. His brain just kept coming up against *baby* and stalling. 'And will you stop saying sorry?'

The absent afterthought made Lara lift her head. 'I can't stand women who cry all the time,' she sniffed, wiping the moisture off her face with the backs of her hands and missing the tender expression that momentarily broke through the shock on Raoul's lean face.

'Here.'

She took the laundered man-sized handkerchief and with a prosaic sniff she straightened her spine and looked into the face that was level with hers. She forgot what she had been about to say as a wave of love washed like a soul-deep sigh over her.

'I know this is the last thing you need right now—I—'

'*We!* It's not as if you didn't have a bit of help.' *When...?* Raoul pushed away the thought. It didn't really matter when it had happened; the way forward was to deal with this reality. He pushed against a crushing tide of guilt—*he* had done this to her.

'It's not really so terrible. I quite like the idea of being a young mother. If you like, I can keep you in touch with what is happening, milestones, you know, the birthdays and—'

'*Keep me in touch...?*'

'If you want?' Was she assuming too much?

'Where do you think I'm going to be?'

She made herself look at him, while struggling for a modicum of composure—better late than never!—and shook her head, not wanting to think about where he might be or, more specifically, with whom.

He dragged her to her feet then slowly but inexorably pulled her towards him until they stood thigh to thigh. 'Has it not occurred to you that I might want this child too?'

'To replace the one she took away?'

He didn't say anything but the words hung between them.

It was Lara who broke the silence. 'No, it hadn't occurred to me,' she admitted honestly. 'How could it? You've just finished telling me that you want to live your life alone.'

'This is about responsibility.'

'Is that all it is to you?' she flung back, wishing as much for him and their unborn child as for herself that it could be more.

'I'm not going to lie to you, Lara, pretend things I do not feel, but I had a no-hope father who always put his own needs ahead of his children's. I will not do that to any child of mine.'

'And if that's not enough…?'

'For who…you?'

'Yes,' she admitted in a quiet voice.

'It might turn out that way,' he admitted. 'But don't you think we should try…for the baby?'

'What do you mean by try? Do you mean that we should stay married? Because that was not part of the plan.'

'Having a baby wasn't part of the plan either,' he retorted.

'I thought you'd be angry.' Weirdly it seemed

to her he was recovering from the shock quicker than she had.

'People *get* married because of babies, they don't get *unmarried*.'

'You wouldn't be suggesting this if there wasn't a baby, would you?'

'No.' She deserved a truthful answer, but she also deserved a man capable of love.

'No.'

Lara tried to tell herself that if he'd lied she would have refused his offer, but she knew she wouldn't. She simply didn't have the strength.

'I've actually come to appreciate what Grandfather meant when he spoke of continuity, of wanting to pass on the name, the genes...'

'Oh, how convenient, now you suddenly *want* a baby? When did this happen? In the last five seconds?'

'I would never have made the conscious choice to have a child.' He would never have brought a child into the world merely to give his life meaning; the selfishness of the idea repelled him. 'But now that I am going to be a father I will be the best one that I can.' It would never be good enough, but luckily for their child he or she would have Lara for a mother to make up for it.

She gasped when, without warning, he placed a hand over her flat stomach.

Lara caught his wrist, felt a rush of emotion and hope. 'You think this could work.'

'We will *make* it work, *cara.*'

CHAPTER TEN

'A WEEKEND?' Raoul's ebony brows almost hit his hairline as he watched Lara close the lid on another suitcase.

Lara turned, her heart skipping a beat as she met his smiling eyes. 'I'm nearly ready. It's not all mine—I have presents for everyone.'

Raoul crossed the room and sat on the bed, causing a pile of neatly folded silky underwear in rainbow colours to slide to the floor. He hooked a provocative thong and swung it on his finger.

'Do you mind? I spent…ooh!'

She landed with a throaty giggle on his lap. Framing her face, he kissed her deeply. When he finally drew back she laid her face on his shoulder, inhaling the warm scent of his skin as she looped her arms around his neck.

She focused on the moment and felt happy, though not totally relaxed. If she did that she might fall off the emotional tightrope that she'd been walking for the last few months. It was simply a matter of focusing on what she had, not on what she longed for. So long as she didn't expect too much, this could work.

And she had a lot to be thankful for: the baby growing inside her, the anticipation of motherhood, which she had never expected to feel so right.

'I need to finish packing.'

Raoul let her disentangle herself and lay back, hands behind his head, watching her finish her packing.

'Won't your mother and sister be hurt you haven't told them until now?' He had fallen in with Lara's decision to keep her pregnancy a secret from everyone including her family, actually *especially* her family, despite the fact it had always made him uneasy.

He still didn't understand it.

He felt the bed give slightly and heard her troubled little hitch of breath as she climbed onto it beside him. She tucked her feet under her as she adopted a kneeling position, looking down on him with her hair falling in a glorious fiery cloud around her face.

'I told you, I'm not ashamed.' She brushed her lips over his then, anchoring her hair with her forearm, and added, 'But I'm not the only one having a baby. Lily is pregnant.' Her sister's due date was approaching fast.

'Then surely that gives you something else in common.' Beyond the fact they were virtually identical to look at. It still bewildered him how his reaction to two women with the same face and body could be so totally different. One made him yawn…no, that wasn't fair, or even strictly true.

Lara's twin sister was not boring, she simply wasn't Lara, who ignited an insatiable desire in him that seemed to bypass every logic circuit.

His feelings for her might go deeper than desire? He pushed away the question, knowing that there was a limit to how many times it would go away unanswered.

How long could he keep dodging the issue?

Was he going to allow Lucy's poison to reach out from the grave and infect his future?

He closed down the internal dialogue—things were all right, better than all right, as they were. Why meddle with something that was working?

'Lily is facing being a single parent. Her situation couldn't be more different than mine and I don't want to make her feel—'

Raoul looped a hand casually around the back of her head, rubbing a caressing thumb across the angle of her jaw. He drew her down, pressing a hard, hungry kiss to her lips.

'You're a good sister.' He landed a kiss on the tip of her nose as she pulled away. Shaking her hair back, she laughed, a hard little sound that drew a frown from Raoul.

'Care to share the joke?'

'I'm not the good twin, that's Lily.'

She turned her head sharply, causing her hair to fall in a concealing curtain across her face. That she didn't want to make Lily feel bad *had* been true and it still was, but the real reason Lara was delaying the moment was not to spare her twin's feeling but her own.

They definitely weren't the type of twins that had some kind of psychic bond, it was just that her sister had the ability to instinctively ask the right questions—all the questions Lara was avoiding. She knew the conversation was inevitable but it was one she wasn't ready to have, or she hadn't been until now.

At the wedding she had kept Lily at arm's length for that very reason. She had known that Lily had been hurt but she also knew that her sister would never understand what she was doing... Who would?

She'd gone away to lose her virginity with one man and ended up falling in love and marrying another, and in the end neither man had loved her even the slightest bit.

Her hungry emerald stare shielded by a heavy fringe of lashes moved over her husband. There was bewilderment mingled in with the need and love that swept over her in a tidal wave of emotion.

The truth, or rather the public lie their relationship was based on, never went away, but there were some days when it remained a whisper in the back of her mind.

Admitting to her twin that their marriage had been a lie from the beginning and the only reason they were together was the baby would turn that whisper into a shout.

And she couldn't bear the thought of Lily looking at her with pity.

Her words were more revealing than she knew. Raoul felt a slug of anger and an image flashed into his head of a younger, more vulnerable Lara being asked why she wasn't more like her sister.

'Just because you've been assigned a role,' he

roughed out softly, 'doesn't mean you have to live up to it.'

Her startled eyes flew to his face. 'Nobody ever did that.' There was defensiveness in the tilt of her chin as she tucked her hair behind her ears.

He angled a sceptical brow. 'I'm not saying it was deliberate.' He tried a different tack. 'Has it occurred to you that you're not so wild and she's not so sensible? Just that you're very different people?' He didn't want to encourage his Lara to compare herself to her twin all the time.

His...?

The possessive trend of his thoughts made him tense. *A figure of speech*, soothed the voice in his head. And what man with an honest breath in his body wouldn't like the idea of Lara being exclusively his?

'You think I'm not so wild?'

Her teasing was rewarded with a lustful growl. He curved a possessive hand across the back of her head and she went with it, allowing her body to fall across him as his mouth moved across hers in a slow, seductive kiss.

Several minutes later she sat back, pink-cheeked and dishevelled. 'I have to finish my packing.'

'What's stopping you?' he asked innocently.

Ten minutes later she clicked closed the lock on her overnight bag and gave a last glance around the room.

'I'll go tell Vincenzo we're ready—*finally.*' He huffed an irritated curse, fished out his phone and, glancing at the caller ID, signalled to Lara to go ahead.

By the time he had joined her she was already ensconced in the back seat of the limo. Raoul slung the case in the open boot and nodded to the driver before he slid in beside her.

He could sense her excitement.

'You miss your family?'

She nodded. 'Yes, I do.' She pressed a hand to her stomach. 'Especially now.'

'Are you all right?'

'Fine.' Lara stretched forward to relive the nagging ache in her back. She had read all the books and she knew this was normal. But she also knew the warmth, the spreading stain were not...

'Raoul...!'

He turned his head in alarm, then slowly followed the direction of her fixed stare.

For a few heart-thudding moments he was paralysed as he stared down at the crimson stain on her skirt and the seat, dripping onto the floor.

Lara whimpered. 'Something's wrong.' It provided the impetus for him to react.

Curling his hand over hers, he turned his head to yell at the driver, who threw the car into a screeching one-eighty-degree turn and set off at speed, ignoring the numerous horn blasts of complaint that followed him.

'Don't worry. Vincenzo drove tanks in the military. We'll have you there in five minutes.' Would five minutes be quick enough? There was so much blood. He looked away from it, focusing on her face, her white, tragic, pain-filled face, while he tried to channel calm.

Inside, Raoul didn't feel calm. He felt an icy fist clawing in his belly, tightening, spreading cold and fear… Could anyone lose that much blood and survive? Of course she could; this wasn't the Dark Ages—women didn't die this way any more. They could transplant hearts and rebuild shattered limbs…but there was so, so much blood!

'Faster!' he flung over his shoulder to Vincenzo, who was already breaking speed limits in a major way.

'Is the baby all right, Raoul…?'

Wishing he could take away the fear in her shadowed eyes, he took her hands between his; they seemed so small and white, and they were cold, so very cold.

He had never felt so helpless in his entire life.

He shook his head. 'Don't talk now, *cara*, save your—No, don't close your eyes, Lara, Lara, stay with me, *cara*.' His voice cracked as he pleaded, 'Stay with me!'

The lashes that lay against her waxen cheeks lifted and Raoul exhaled a gasp of relief. 'I've made such a mess of your lovely car.'

He swore with soft, savage fluency and lifted her hands to his lips, kissing her individual fingertips. 'I'll send you the bill.' He lifted his head in response to the driver's voice. 'We're here!' he said to Lara, whose eyes had begun to flutter closed once more. 'Everything will be all right, just hold on.'

'Who do you think you are? You can't park here! This space is reserved for ambulance emergencies.'

Raoul responded to the officious instructions in the same language, slicing out in a steel monotone, 'Can't you see it *is* an emergency? Get me a doctor! Now!'

Any inclination to argue the point faded as Raoul emerged and his interrogator saw Lara, who was drifting in and out of consciousness. He turned and shouted; in response two figures and a trolley appeared. They had transferred Lara to it when a doctor arrived and began to take charge.

The questions he shot at Raoul were reassuringly concise and to the point. In comparison, his own response seemed painfully slow as his tongue struggled to keep pace with his brain.

'I'm afraid you can't go beyond this point. Please take a seat.'

At the prospect of Lara being wheeled through those big double doors, away from him, something close to panic slid though Raoul. Then, as if she sensed what he was feeling, the little hand in his tightened and Raoul shook his head, barely recognising his own voice as he responded, 'No, I will not.'

The comment didn't throw the nurse, who made the request more firmly but still politely. She gave an understanding smile that made him want to yell at her—he didn't want smiles, he wanted someone to do something.

'I'm afraid, sir, that you—'

Raoul was afraid too, very afraid as the fingers in his suddenly went limp.

'Lara!' His yell of anguish diverted attention from him to Lara. It seemed to him that she was barely breathing. 'Do something!'

They *were* doing things, pushing him out of the way to get to the unconscious figure. When the doors swung shut moments later, leaving him standing the wrong side, he didn't move. He just stood there, hands clenched and white at his sides, feeling the weight of paralysing helplessness bearing down on him.

Raoul had lost count of the number of people who had walked through the door but on each successive occasion he braced himself only to experience a massive anticlimax as they walked on by. He was pretty much resigned for more of the same when a tall, grey-haired figure still wearing scrubs pushed the door open.

The man walked straight up to him and held out his hand. The grasp was reassuringly strong. 'I'm your wife's surgeon. She came through the operation well.'

It wasn't until the older man released his hand that Raoul realised his own was shaking. The screaming tension that held his body rigid released itself in a slow sibilant sigh.

The man looked at him with sympathy. 'You must have questions.'

'It happened so quickly.'

The doctor inclined his head. 'If you'd like to come through to my office…?'

Lara was dimly aware of being moved from the car to the trolley, but it all had a nightmarish quality. But the nightmare was not real, not while she had hold of Raoul's hand. So she held on tight as she was whisked along corridors, aware of the blur of faces, the glare of lights overhead hurting her eyes, hearing snatches of the buzz of conversation going on around her.

Then there was just black.

'No, leave it, Lara.' Fingers cool and firm stopped her pulling at the thing taped to her hand.

She knew the voice, the touch; she opened her eyes and Raoul was still holding her hand.

She was grateful he didn't wait for her to ask.

'They couldn't save the baby.'

She had known already, but hearing it made it real. 'What did I do wrong?'

It was not the response that he had anticipated

but before Raoul could react to it a figure strolled into the room. The scrubs were gone and he was dressed in an open-necked shirt; it was only the badge he wore and the stethoscope protruding from his pocket that pronounced his medical status.

'You did nothing, Mrs Di Vittorio,' the doctor said firmly in his perfect English. 'Many mothers experience irrational guilt after a miscarriage.' He addressed his remark to Raoul and, after glancing at the chart at the foot of Lara's bed, walked around to stand closer to her head.

'And there was nothing you could have done to prevent it.'

'But I was nearly twenty weeks. I thought after the first twelve—'

'Miscarriages in the second trimester are not as common as those in the early weeks,' he agreed gently. 'But they do happen.'

'Why?' Lara forced the question past the aching occlusion in her throat.

'Many reasons. In your case, I'm afraid that the baby actually died a little time ago...'

'No!' Adrenaline of denial giving her a surge of strength, Lara struggled into a sitting position, wincing as the needle in her arm caught in her hair as she pushed it out of her face.

'It's not possible, I'd have known!'

The doctor placed a compassionate hand on her arm and, watching him, Raoul thought, *He knows what to do, so why don't I?*

She wouldn't be here now if he hadn't dragged her into his life. It had all been about him and his needs; his motivations had all been selfish and this was the result. Self-loathing tightened in his gut. She was better off without him.

'Did you have a bleed…something slight per-haps?'

Lara looked at him blankly for a moment and then blinked. 'No…yes…' She nodded, remem-bering the morning… If she had told someone, sought medical advice and not just put her symp-toms into a search engine, maybe her baby would be alive.

The combined weight of *what if*s and guilt felt as if it were crushing her.

'As I have explained to your husband, you had what is termed a failed miscarriage. The compli-cation came when an infection took hold, which caused the haemorrhage. Luckily we caught you before sepsis set in—that could have been very serious indeed. Look, I'll leave you two to talk, but not for long. You need to rest and, as I told your husband, all being well you can go home in the morning.'

Lara watched the door close; the gentle click echoed in her brain, over and over.

'I don't feel anything,' she said, dropping her head back on the pillow.

'They gave you pain relief, I think.'

'No, not that sort of feeling.' She pressed a hand to her chest. 'I don't feel anything.' She emphasised, 'I'm empty, it's like a vacuum.'

His eyes met hers, and the expression in them was guarded. Without warning, anger rushed into the vacuum she had spoken of, bubbling up.

'Say what you're thinking. You might as well, because it's obvious. The only reason we're together was the baby and now there is no baby, so there's no reason for us to be together any more. Don't worry, I'm not going to make a scene!' she shrilled, to the private room, empty but for the two of them, before her eyes filled with tears.

The sight made Raoul surge forward but Lara held up her hands as if to ward him off as she hissed, 'Don't you dare feel sorry for me!'

Raoul subsided back into the chair pulled up

beside the bed and dragged a hand through his dark hair. 'I feel sorry...no, sad for *us*.' And it was true—alongside the guilt that he carried like a second skin there was a sense of profound loss.

His response threw her, but only for a moment before she shook her head and choked out bitterly, 'There *is* no us. You're probably glad this happened!'

'Don't be ridiculous! I appreciate that I wasn't the one who...the one who...' *Came close to losing my life.* He couldn't say the words but the acknowledgement of it added another layer to his guilt. 'The one who went through the physical trauma, but the baby was mine too. We will both grieve, so doesn't it make sense to you that we go through it together?' It was a logical response, he told himself. 'Who is better placed than me to know what you're feeling?'

Her lips quivered. 'I never thought I'd feel this way, but I wanted this baby... I *really* wanted this baby and it's fine, I don't expect you to understand.'

'I wanted this baby too.'

'Because you feel responsible, that's all.'

'I don't want to be the last Di Vittorio. I have been surrounded by so much death and misery.

A baby… I have been able to look into the future for the first time in years.'

'I didn't know you felt that way…'

He gave an odd laugh. 'Neither did I. Look, life has kicked you, Lara, but you are strong, you will recover. I really don't think you should make any decisions until then. Let me take care of you.' *It's the least you can do*, mocked the voice in his head, *considering it's your fault she's lying there.*

'And when will that be?'

'I wish I could tell you.'

'And what then?' she asked dully, thinking that if they were going to split up anyway, if he was just waiting until she was stronger, what was the point? She'd never be *that* strong. It was always going to hurt, so why not get the hurting over in one go?

'That depends on what you want. The doctor says there is no reason we can't try again.'

'You're suggesting…'

'I'm suggesting we wait and see. Or would you rather go home to your family?'

Lara thought about seeing her sister with a healthy baby growing inside and shook her head.

'And if it makes you feel better to yell at me,

blame me, that's fine. We will move on, and next time things—'

'Next time if we…things could go wrong again.'

The fear in her voice felt like a hand tearing at his chest.

'It's too soon, just focus on getting better.'

She didn't hear him. Lara was sound asleep.

The next morning, packed and waiting when he arrived, she was speaking on the phone. Conscious he was listening, she wound the conversation up as quickly as possible. 'Bye, Mum, and sorry, speak soon, give my love to Lily.'

'So when is she coming?'

Lara didn't meet his eyes. 'She isn't,' she said brightly.

He tensed. 'So you are going there?' He was afraid that if she went, she might not come back.

Raoul's philosophy in life had always been simple: predict possible outcomes before they happen and plan accordingly. It had helped him survive his marriage from hell and now, for the first time, he could think of no plans, not one. Denial was the only option.

'No.' This response was even less distinct.

What the hell was going on? 'Lara, will you look at me?'

With a heavy sigh Lara lifted her head, shaking back the curtain of burnished hair. 'Don't look at me like that. If you must know, I haven't told her.'

Raoul, who had been reaching into his pocket to switch off his own vibrating phone, let his hand fall away and just stared at her.

'You haven't told her?' She couldn't possibly mean what it sounded like.

'Well, I hadn't told her I was pregnant, so I could hardly tell her I'd lost a baby she didn't know existed.'

She screwed up her mouth, digging her teeth into her full lower lip as she pushed her hair behind her ears. The motion drew attention to the plaster on the back of her hand; the sight of it was an unwelcome reminder of the events of yesterday.

The flash of exasperation that tautened his sculpted features gave way to something between panic and tenderness as he watched a tear trace its way down her pale, smooth cheek.

Lara brushed the moisture away angrily and yelled, 'Don't look at me like that. It's my decision and if you go behind my back and tell them I'll never ever forgive you!' Her chest heaving with the strength of the emotions that were tearing her apart, she poked a finger at him and added a quivering postscript, 'I mean it, Raoul!'

'So I see.'

Anger she could have dealt with, but the half-quizzical smile that suggested he was pleased she was yelling at him drove a stake through her carefully crafted façade, cracking it wide open.

'Lily won't tell me who the father is, so she's keeping secrets too.' The hurt she hadn't even admitted to herself quivered in Lara's voice and she rubbed her hands up and down her upper arms.

Raoul pulled off the jacket he was wearing and laid it across her shoulders, not fighting the impulse that made him kiss the top of her glossy, burnished head.

Lara lifted her head and sniffed. Her beautiful eyes were red-rimmed and swimming, her full lips quivering. 'I w-want to be happy for her.' She swallowed hard and bit her lip. 'But I'm not a nice person. I just keep thinking, why should she get a baby and not me...why my baby...?' She bent her head again and covered her face with her hands, mumbling through her fingers, 'I must be a bad person.'

Her muffled words threatened to break through his control. Holding her would make him feel one hell of a lot better, but was it what she needed at the moment?

'Self-pity,' he drawled, 'doesn't suit you, *cara*. That's better,' he approved warmly when her hands fell away and she shot him a teary but angry glare. 'I'm sorry that things are not good between you and your sister,' he added softly.

She sniffed and explained with husky, hard-won composure, 'I miss… I mean, I don't know what she's thinking or anything but we never used to hide things from one another, we shared.' She gave a loud sniff and made a pathetic attempt to smile that just about broke his heart. 'You don't want to hear this.'

It was true, he didn't, because he didn't enjoy feeling guilty. A major contributing factor in the situation that had led to the deterioration in the relationship between Lara and her twin must have been his insistence she not divulge the true circumstances behind their marriage. Hell, who was he kidding? This was his doing!

Since he'd walked into Lara's life he'd done nothing but cause her heartbreak and pain.

'If you like I could speak to her?'

'You!' Her incredulity at the casual offer was almost as great as Raoul's own. 'What would you say?'

He stayed silent because quite frankly he didn't have a clue and he had no idea what had driven him to make such a pointless gesture.

How about guilt?

'There's been no falling out as such…it'll be fine,' she insisted dully. 'I'm just feeling a bit fragile.'

'You're allowed.' His jaw clenched.

The trouble with Lara was she didn't cut herself any slack. Plus, she never asked for help, which, combined with her bloody-minded attitude, meant that if you did make a suggestion she was pretty much guaranteed to do the opposite. A 'no comment' policy was the safest bet—though not always the most fun.

A quiet life was overrated.

His half-smile faded as he realised what he was doing—remembering make-up sex when she was some place close to hell. *You're a shallow bastard*, he thought.

Yes, she could be a total pain, outspoken, bolshie, opinionated…but he would have welcomed being on the receiving end of any or all of these undesirable qualities if it meant banishing the haunted look from her eyes.

Lara shook her head. 'Look, I know it's fashionable but I really don't need talking therapy.'

She had already rejected the clinic's offer to put her in contact with a grief counsellor. She really couldn't see how talking about something so personal, exposing her innermost feelings to a total stranger, would make anything better. No, Lara thought, she would do what she always had done with painful emotions and memories—she was going to build a great wall, shut them behind it and get on with her life.

'I just want to go home.'

CHAPTER ELEVEN

LARA REMEMBERED THE first time she had walked into the entrance hall of the *palazzo* and got her first impression of the grandeur and history of the ancient building. Her voice had echoed around the vaulted ceiling while Raoul's ancestors had looked down at her from the stone walls with varying degrees of disapproval.

She'd bumped into a suit of armour and tried to pretend she wasn't daunted, but she had been, even though she had grown up in the shadow of a very different but equally impressive historic house where her parents had worked, and where her mum was still housekeeper.

Today as she walked in, the smell of the hospital still lingering on her clothes, the stone walls lined with priceless tapestries felt like a haven. They felt like home.

When had that happened?

'What are these?'

'I have no idea,' Raoul admitted, walking

across the room ahead of her to the items arranged on the heavily carved and inlaid table that took centre stage.

He turned and waved her to the table. 'For you.'

'Me?'

He watched the emotions on her face as she moved along the line, looking at one gift and then the next. She turned back to him holding the bouquet of prize roses grown by the *palazzo*'s head gardener, a surly, monosyllabic individual who grew them for the horticultural event he won every year—the blooms were normally off-limits to everyone.

She closed her eyes and inhaled the heady fragrance. 'Marguerite has cooked me my favourite biscuits, those lovely little almond ones.' Her throat closed over with emotion as she picked up an offering she had missed, a glossy magazine tied with a fluorescent bow.

'Rosa,' she said with a smile even before she glanced at the attached card.

'Who is Rosa?'

'One day she'll be famous, but right now she helps in the kitchen. She's halfway through a fine arts degree. I pass on my magazines to her.'

Small wonder she was so popular with the staff.

In the comparatively short time she had been here Lara had come to know more about the people who lived and worked on the estate than he did.

'Everyone is so kind.'

'It would seem you have won their hearts.'

Lara looked away, burying her face in the roses before he could see the truth she knew was written on her face—there was only one heart she was interested in winning and that belonged to someone else.

If she couldn't have his heart, she could have his baby; she could give the man she loved that at least.

'Were you serious?' She fixed him with a grave questioning stare. 'Do you want to try again?'

'I do.'

The admission had been a long time coming.

Since Lucy he had not allowed himself to think about a family, not even when his grandfather had brought up the subject. A family came with love; you couldn't have one without the other. The logic was inescapable.

Almost having a child by accident had exposed the lie: he wanted an heir, a child…and he wanted it with Lara, who did not ask him for things he could not give.

'But maybe now is not the time to think about it.'

'I have thought.' She tipped her head up. 'I think I'd like that.'

'That is not a decision to make now. We will discuss this later.'

'When later?'

'You're asking me to give you a date?'

She pressed her lips together.

'Even if you do know your own mind, your body needs time to recover. If you still feel the same way in a year...'

'A year!' she yelped.

'All right, nine months.'

'I won't change my mind,' she said, thinking, *but you might.*

Raoul stood a little apart from the family group as Lara embraced her mother and then her twin, bending a head to brush her lips across the forehead of the baby. For someone who was looking for it, all the sadness and pain she had been struggling to hide all day under a bright, bubbly exterior was there glistening in her eyes.

Watching, helpless to do a damned thing, he felt as if a blunt knife were twisting in his stomach… Surely they *must* see…? But no, her twin and her mother were both focused on the baby.

He didn't know whether to applaud or weep when, a moment later, Lara was smiling, back in control and giving an Oscar-worthy performance of the self-absorbed, wild-child sister, and all the time crying inside.

'Well, rather you than me, Lily.' She laughed, patting her flat stomach with a complacent smile that made it seem as if she had nothing more to worry about in the world than her waistline. 'I don't fancy having to change my wardrobe.'

How often had she hidden her feelings this way in the past? he wondered? Maybe she wasn't so easy to read after all? He had debated whether to invent an urgent appointment and bring this visit to a premature end, but he was glad now that they had stayed longer. Not that Lara would have broken down, she was too determined to appear thrilled for her sister, but if he had to watch her being bright and smiley while her heart was breaking for another second…he doubted he would be able to fulfil his promise of silence on the subject of her miscarriage.

'I can't get over how much she's grown,' Lara

said, retrieving a toy that had been tossed on the floor.

'They usually do in a year,' her twin responded quietly.

The stricken look that slid across Lara's face could have been caused by the undertone in her twin's voice, or the reminder of the previous visit, right after the birth, when Lara had insisted on flying over to see her sister.

Only a couple of weeks after her own miscarriage. Raoul had tried his best to dissuade her, but in the end she'd threatened to catch a flight on her own, so he'd taken her.

It had been a nightmare. Oh, Lara had managed to say all the right things at the hospital, had held the baby and told her sister how clever she was, but outside she had virtually collapsed in a heap.

She had sobbed uncontrollably on the flight back and pretty much for the next two days. Since then she had made excuses whenever a visit home was suggested, until today.

'Goodbye, Emily Rose, be good for Mummy.'

The baby, who was dressed in a cute pink outfit that she was almost too big for at eleven months, grabbed for Lara's hair.

'No, Emmy.' Lily clicked her tongue and detached the chubby fingers.

From where he was standing Raoul could see the muscles in Lara's pale throat working as she straightened up. Even someone with an armour-plated heart could not have failed to be moved by her struggle for control. He might not agree with her decision to keep the miscarriage a secret, but it was *her* decision, and he had to respect that. However wrong, misguided and pig-headed he thought she was being.

He cleared his throat and glanced pointedly at the time that blinked on the screen of his phone. 'I'm sorry to break up the party and drag you away, but we're on the clock here.'

It worked. Lara's twin and mother looked at her with sympathy and him with a lack of it—which was fine by Raoul. He was not seeking either their sympathy or approval.

He placed a hand on Lara's elbow and, projecting a level of callous impatience that he hoped was consistent with someone heartless and controlling—after all, was it a million miles from his actual character?—he raised his voice once more to be heard above the whirr of the blades of the waiting helicopter.

'Ladies.' He tipped his head curtly and pulled Lara, skipping along on her spiky heels to keep up with him, towards the door. She still retained her grip on his arm, though she no longer needed his support.

Behind them the two women exchanged worried glances.

Once they took off and the figures below vanished from view, Lara released a long shuddering sigh and leaned back, her eyes closed.

Sitting opposite her, Raoul sat waiting.

'There is no urgent appointment, is there?'

'No.'

She opened her eyes, which were luminescent with tears. 'I could have coped.'

'I'm sure you could,' he returned smoothly. 'But I probably wouldn't have if we'd stayed any longer.'

She shook her head as if the idea the day had been anything other than a breeze for him had not occurred to her. 'It was lovely to see everyone.'

People she missed…a life she regretted leaving behind? He pushed the thought away. 'Everyone said how lovely the baby was.'

He arched a brow at her quick defence. 'And nobody, not a soul, mentioned the father.'

Eyes wide with horror, she leaned forward in her seat. 'You didn't…?'

'What, after you told me the subject was off-limits? I wouldn't dare.'

She gave a disbelieving grunt and settled back in her seat.

'But the strain of not mentioning the elephant in the room was beginning to tell.'

'Lily hasn't told anyone.' *Not even me.* 'Raoul…? It's been nearly a year now, and I haven't changed my mind.'

Though she had been angry at the time, she was grateful now that he had insisted on the wait. For the last few months her emotions had been all over the place.

She knew she hadn't been easy to live with but Raoul had been incredibly patient, when she got angry with him, herself or life in general. And then there had been the sad times when all she could do was cry.

'Today—'

'Today was hard,' she admitted. 'Inside,' she said, pressing a hand to her chest, 'I feel like a mother but no one can see that. One day I hurt, the next I feel as if it had happened to someone else. I know I've been hell to live with and that was never part of the contract.'

'I broke the contract when I got you pregnant.'

'So your guilt is keeping us together.' She turned to stare at the clouds.

He wished he could have said yes, that would have made things simpler to sort in his own mind, but though guilt played a part there was a lot more keeping him with Lara, more than he wanted to think about.

'A little while back I thought you'd changed your mind… Was I wrong?'

She turned her head and looked at him in astonishment. 'For a while,' she admitted, 'I did feel as though having another baby would be betraying the one I lost… I suppose that sounds mad to you.'

'No, it doesn't.'

Her eyes slid from his and she looked out of the window. 'It might never happen for us.'

He responded with an emotion-dampening positivity. 'Of course it will, and if it doesn't it won't be for lack of trying.'

'So you haven't changed your mind?'

His libido gave a lazy kick as she relaxed and

laughed again; the sound made him realise how rare these moments were now.

'I want...' He wanted to see her happy, he wanted to repair the damage he had wrought after watching what she had been through during the last year. He would have done anything to make her laugh like that again. 'No,' he said softly.

'How about it, then...?' Holding his interested gaze, she slipped off her spiky heels and, tongue caught between her teeth in sexy concentration, her green eyes wide and mockingly innocent, she stretched out her bare foot and moved it slowly up his leg.

'You think...?'

He felt the heat rising up his neck, then the heat coalesced a little lower as her foot came to rest between his thighs. 'In a helicopter, *really*...?'

Eyes dancing, she gave a wicked chuckle and withdrew her foot. 'Well, maybe it can wait until the plane... I mean, what's the use of having a private jet if you can't make use of the privacy?'

'I like the way your mind works,' he said, thinking now this was the way babies should be made!

CHAPTER TWELVE

Eight months later

IT HAD BEEN Lara's idea to revive the masked ball that had last been held at the *palazzo* twenty years before. If anyone had asked him his opinion, and they hadn't, Raoul would have pointed to the high wall that surrounded the property and said it had been built for a reason—to keep people out.

But she was so fired up about it that he hadn't been able to bring himself to throw a damper on her enthusiasm. His agreement to the scheme had been taken as read, though there had been several times since when he'd wished he had objected, not least when an army of caterers, musicians and assorted staff who were required for the smooth running of such a social event invaded his home.

Still, it looked as if the hard work had paid off. The night seemed to be a roaring success.

Raoul could hear his wife's throaty laugh from

across the room. Her head was thrown back to reveal the lovely line of her swan-like throat, and the emeralds that had been dug out of the vault for the occasion lay glinting against the pearlescent skin of her breasts. That had been their first row tonight—the dress too revealing, too everything.

His thoughts slid back to when she had walked through from her dressing room carrying his mask in one hand, hers in the other.

The cut of the black dress had drawn a spontaneous low, feral groan from his throat; once he had started breathing again all he could think about was peeling it off.

'You can't wear that!'

In retrospect Raoul could see that he could have dealt with the situation better, but then hindsight was a marvellous thing.

The smile left her lovely face and her chin went up as she tossed his mask across. He lifted a hand automatically to catch it.

'You want to dictate what I wear?'

Hell, there was the *quiet voice*, the one that generally preceded a redheaded meltdown. He felt an answering flare of temper aggravated by extreme sexual frustration.

'Do you always have to get your own way?' he countered, thinking of all the times he had let her have it. *You're in danger of turning into a lapdog, Raoul.*

'Have you ever heard of compromise? Or patience?'

'I *beg* your pardon! And if I am a male, controlling jerk for wanting my wife not to wear something that could get her arrested—'

Her magnificent eyes flashed green fire up at him and her even more magnificent bosom swelled with wrath. 'You think I look like a hooker?'

'Do not put words in my mouth.'

'It's not my fault if some men have one-track minds!'

Raoul hooked a hand around her back and felt a deep responsive quiver run through her body as she dropped the hand-painted antique mask. 'I'm not *some* men, I am your husband.' The argument, the real cause, the hundreds of guests about to arrive burned away in seconds as the heat of primitive need consumed him.

'Shall I help you out of it…?'

He took her throaty little whimper as a yes and started to slide the zipper of the scandalous dress down. The image in his head of it falling in a silken puddle at her feet vanished as she suddenly stiffened and pulled away and, with hands raised above her head, began to struggle frantically to pull the zipper back up.

'You think all you have to do is get me in bed and I'll agree to anything!' she charged furiously.

Nerve-shredding frustration gnawed at him as he walked towards her. His control was perilously close to snapping. It must have been reflected on his face because Lara, matching his steps, backed away until her back was pressed into the canopy of their four-poster bed.

'It's getting you there, *cara*, that can be problematic.'

'You arrogant—' she gasped, her voice vanishing as they faced one another, panting, their mingled breaths crystallising into an electrical charge that vibrated in the air around them.

'Lara, I'm—'

She was leaning into him, her luscious lips a breath away from his, when a loud tap on the door made her blink like someone waking.

'Come in!' she yelled, before adding a warning, 'Hush!' as Raoul swore.

'Sorry to disturb you, but the caterers have a

problem with the ice sculptures. They say they can't work with—'

Raoul's groan drowned out the rest of the woman's words. He didn't have a clue who she was but he'd seen her about the place the past week.

Lara shot him a cold glance. 'Don't worry, Sara, I'll come and have a word, just give me a moment, would you?' She waited until the door shut before she rounded on Raoul. 'Do you have to be so rude?'

'Me!'

'Yes, you! Would it kill you to smile? You make her nervous.'

'I don't seem to make you nervous.'

'You make me—!' She gave a little gasp that drowned out whatever it was she was going to say.

He found his anger shifting, giving way to reluctant concern as he realised how fragile she was looking. Her make-up might hide the shadows underneath her incredible eyes but it didn't disguise the sharpness of her delicately carved collarbones.

'Have you ever heard of delegation?'

Her determination to be involved in every aspect of this charity ball meant that there had been times when he had made time to be with her, and, rather than appreciate the effort he was making, she'd stood him up, for a florist! Oh, and, how could he have forgotten? A bottled-water supplier!

He liked to think his ego was fairly resistant but rain check…?

It wasn't that he felt neglected, it was not as though he expected her to be at his beck and call—the idea was laughable—but the dark shadows under her eyes were not. But as much as Raoul found the entire thing a pain, he couldn't help but admire the way she'd thrown herself into it.

But then, that was Lara. She never did anything at less than full throttle, he brooded, floating a glance over her sleek, sexy outfit. His opinion that the outfit was not fit for public consumption did not stop his blood heating and his body hardening. He frowned, imagining that he wouldn't be the only man she had this effect on tonight.

'What are you going to do, serve the soup and conduct the orchestra?'

His disdain brought an angry flush to Lara's cheeks. Not breaking eye contact, she lifted her chin to a determined angle. 'I want everything to be perfect. Would it have been too much to expect a little support?'

She had no intention of admitting that there had been many times when she'd wished she'd never started it.

Even if the person she was doing it for wasn't impressed… She blinked away the thought. This wasn't about impressing anyone, this was about charity.

'Why? What does it matter? People will get drunk and say things they regret the next morning. You're not being judged. It's all in your mind,' he said, tapping his own head.

'You just criticised the way I look.' She took a step towards him and lifted her chin. 'I'd call that judging, *caro*.'

She curled her fingers around the ornate handle of her mask and held it up. It covered the upper half of her face, leaving her lush, crimson-painted lips and rounded chin visible while through the slits her eyes sparkled like the green gems around her neck.

'I may not be able to make a baby but I can damned well organise a party!' Her defiance melted away as her words hung there in the air between them.

She was acting as though she'd just made some great reveal. But Lara was not telling Raoul anything he didn't already know. The timing had said it all. She had picked up the masked-ball baton and hit the ground running a day after their last big fight about IVF.

With a sigh, Lara dropped her hand. What good was there in hiding behind a mask when she'd just volunteered all her insecurities? Thanks to her big mouth. It would take more than some papier mâché to hide them now.

The siren had vanished, her face stripped bare of provocation; it was impossible not to feel her pain.

'Nobody has said you…we…can't have a baby.' He had humoured her with the tests but he might as well not have bothered. They had been given the all-clear, but every month her wild optimism gave way to dark depression. The cycle was relentless.

'Then why hasn't it happened?'

He closed his eyes at the constant cry. 'Maybe,' he ground out, 'because you are constantly so uptight! Relax and forget about it for a minute, stop taking your temperature every five minutes. Stop obsessing about getting pregnant and it might happen.'

Lara compressed her lips. Easy for him to say. He wasn't the one waiting for someone to call time on the marriage if she failed. It would be easy for him, he had no emotional investment in it, he could just shrug and walk away, find someone else to continue the genetic line. It was *his* line, not hers, that was important here.

She was not denying that he had put time and effort into their marriage, more than she had expected if she was honest, but he hadn't put his heart into it.

But she couldn't cry foul. She'd known what she was getting into, had agreed to it all with her eyes open, and he had never pretended he wanted anything other than a baby. The voice of reason in her head made her fling out bitterly, 'I'm not even sure you have a heart!'

This seemingly disconnected and unreasonable accusation made his sympathy shrivel and his paper-thin patience come closer to vanishing totally as he drawled, 'I didn't think it was my heart you were interested in.'

The irony of complaining about being treated like a sex object by a gorgeous and desirable woman was not wasted on him. He was sure that most men would envy his position and while there were many plus points—he had no problem with the fact that she couldn't seem to get enough of him, that she melted at his touch—he couldn't quite rid himself of the suspicion that was nagging at the back of his mind: was her desire real, or was it just the right time of her cycle?

You're just never satisfied, are you, Di Vittorio? What the hell do you want—love...? On that grounding mental observation he took a deep breath and decided to be reasonable. He might even wear the damned mask!

'Anyone would think you'd like for me to fail!'

Reason forgotten, he'd chucked his mask out of the window and hadn't responded to the accusation. To do so would have been to throw himself into an emotional minefield.

Instead, he had let her leave, her sweeping exit only spoiled by the fact that she'd had to come back for her shoes, which rather ruined the dramatic effect.

As he thought back on it now the memory twitched his lips into a half-smile that flattened out as the internationally renowned singer came to the end of the number she had been belting out, and above the applause that followed another peal of husky laughter reached him.

He swore, causing several of the nearest masked faces to turn.

Great, now he was the one raising brows while his wife flirted with just about every man in the room. Well, enough was enough!

On the specially constructed stage, the singer took another bow and in turn applauded the musicians. Raoul tuned out her voice as she bent to the microphone and explained why one of the charities this event was raising money for was so close to her heart.

That had been the response to his every negative comment about this event—*but it's for charity*.

On stage, the singer went on to speak of a change in mood that brought a spatter of anticipatory applause. He craned his neck to catch sight of his Lara. Ice slid into his eyes as he stared over the heads of people at his wife just as the guy she was with leaned in to say something in her ear. Raoul recognised him as the son of a media tycoon whose idea of a day's work was giving an interview to a magazine about the stress involved in being him.

Raoul could recall being seated next to him at a dinner once and having been narcoleptic with boredom before the main course was served.

Not that Lara seemed bored. Her eyes sparkled, the emeralds sparkled, the guy touched her arm…and he heard a snapping noise in his head. Blood pounding in his ears, he crossed the room, his progress impeded by the fact that manners meant he couldn't just push his guests out of the way.

He responded with a grunt to a couple of greetings and then the effort became too much and he adopted a selective deafness policy.

Lara laughed, even though she hadn't actually heard the punchline of the joke. She was really working hard at this hostess thing but, heaven help her, there were limits. This man was monumentally boring.

'Sorry, duty calls.' Lies were a lot easier when you had a mask to hide behind.

It was odd, but the more miserable she felt, the easier it became to laugh and act as if she were having a great time. And she *would* have a great time, she told herself, even if it killed her, which it just might. Or perhaps Raoul might—In the periphery of her vision she could see his dark head as he made his way towards her.

Across the sea of faces their eyes met. He was the only person in the room *not* wearing a mask, and as their glances connected she was very glad of her own to hide behind. Something close to panic broke free as he continued to weave his way through their guests. He not only moved with the elegance of a jungle cat, but he projected the same lethal grace you associated with that animal. It was all she could do not to run.

Lara took a deep breath, told herself she was being ridiculous, and turned back to the boring man who still hadn't got to the punchline of his next story. She struggled to pick up the thread of his conversation while wondering how this young man managed to say so much without actually saying anything at all.

Raoul reached her side just as the band struck up the opening bars of the famous hit. An expectant hush descended on the room as all eyes turned to the stage. Though not quite all eyes.

Raoul's were on her.

Raoul extended an arm towards Lara. 'My dance, I think.' He slid a look towards the other man who had faded away in Lara's mind the moment Raoul appeared, and in fact was already backing away looking distinctly uneasy.

Lara didn't blame him. If a wolf could smile it would have copied Raoul's.

'I don't want to dance.'

The singer's husky, mellow tones filled the room as couples around them began to gyrate and twirl.

'And I don't care what you want. This is about what I want.'

She pulled in a tense breath as he tugged her into his arms. He was an excellent dancer and she was swept along by the slow, sexy beat of the music and the thrill of being in his arms—that part never lessened. Lara wasn't aware of his intention until he danced her straight out of one of the big double doors that had been thrown open earlier.

The ribbons attached to her mask fluttered in the breeze as they stepped outside.

She spun around to face him, still clutching the exotic mask to her face. 'Will you take that damned thing off?' He took hold of her wrist and pulled the mask down, anchoring her arm to her side and jerking her towards him.

Without her shield Lara felt exposed under the ravaging intensity of his glittering stare.

'*Dio*, but you're so beautiful.'

She felt him shudder, a deep ripple of movement that exploded through his body.

His mouth, not hard but sensuous, his firm lips warm and seductive, moved over hers, his tongue sliding between her parted lips. When his dark head lifted his intense stare made her dizzy.

'Raoul, you can't, people are staring.'

'Can't a man kiss his wife?'

There was kissing and there was *kissing*, and that had definitely been the latter!

'I'm jealous.'

The abrupt declaration made her stare. He had never said anything like that to her before.

'Wasn't I meant to be?'

The question made her eyes wide. She opened her mouth to hotly deny the question and closed it again. Wasn't there an element of truth in what he said?

'You don't make me sound like a very nice person,' she returned, hurt quivering in her voice.

'I don't want nice! I want not to be pushed away, treated like the enemy. We do not seem to be making each other happy, Lara.'

Lara felt the tears press at the back of her throat. 'The only place we don't fight is in bed.'

She took a deep breath, her hostility falling away as she felt a sob rise in her throat. She had always known this would happen, she just hadn't expected it to be here, now.

'So you are saying you want a divorce? I think you might have chosen a less public place.'

'This is not a public place, it is my home.'

'You didn't want any of this, did you? I knew it and I still went ahead and—I'm sorry.' *Just like the baby.* 'I just wanted to do something that *I* could control…and if I don't fill the time I think about—' She lifted her hand to her head. 'It just doesn't stop.'

'I understand,' he said gently. 'I really do, but, Lara, we have to get on the same page with this thing. After all we both want the same thing, don't we? I don't want a divorce.'

Thinking of the way she'd been behaving, Lara wondered why not.

Raoul stood there wondering the same thing himself. What had happened to his safe compartmentalised life?

'Couldn't we take a day off from the baby thing? Does it have to dominate *everything*?'

Of course it had to dominate everything—it was the only reason they were together. Lara bit her tongue to stop herself blurting it out.

'I suppose so, but this is—'

'I know, for charity.'

'I'm sorry, I really am, I just got carried away, the dress...' The truth was she had not felt comfortable with so much flesh exposed all night.

'Are your hostess duties over for the evening?'

'Pretty much.'

'Then how about we slip away and have our own little party?'

'I'd like that.'

CHAPTER THIRTEEN

'CHARLES THINKS IT will be a good year, a vintage year. He also said he doesn't need a new assistant because you do more than the one he had. Should I put you on the payroll?'

'It's interesting,' she admitted.

Hot after the walk to the vineyard manager's office, Lara turned her face into the light breeze, though with Raoul standing there with his shirt open to the waist, a section of brown skin on show and the silver buckle of his jeans shining against the hair-roughened skin of his taut, flat belly, there was not much chance of her cooling down.

'The clearing-up operation should be done by now. We made a lot of money if that's any—'

'Forget about last night.'

There were parts Lara didn't want to forget. She pulled at the neck of her shirt as he tipped the remnants of the water bottle he'd been drinking from over his head.

Oh, my! She closed her eyes, willed her galloping hormones to get back in their box.

The sound of him crushing the empty water bottle between his fingers brought her eyes open. There were strands of glossy, wet hair plastered across his forehead and his shirt was splodged with moisture.

He raised a hand and pushed the wet hair off his face and, hooking one thumb into the belt of his jeans, nodded. 'That tree over there—I was six and Jamie was eight when we carved our names into the trunk.'

Her throat filled as she watched him stare into the distance as though he was seeing the day from his past.

'He cut his hand when he cut his name because I was pushing, trying to see.' Then, still staring at the tree, he seamlessly changed the subject. 'I will need to be in New York quite a lot over the next few months.'

'New York?'

'Yes, I had thought I could keep up the law side of things but it's not going to work. I'm selling up. I can delegate the satellite offices but I need to see through the New York handover myself as there are still outstanding commitments that need to be honoured.'

'I suppose that will mean a lot of travelling?' And a lot of nights alone.

'It could,' he agreed. 'But there are alternatives.'

She shook her head, suddenly sure what was coming next. He had decided to cut his losses.

'We could move there. I have a place.'

She opened her eyes. 'You want me to come with you?'

'I think a break would do you…us…good right now maybe? Look, I know it's easy for me to talk about changing the cycle, but maybe a physical move would help? And while we're there, the best IVF specialist in the world is based there…'

'What are you saying, Raoul?' Her heart lurched with wild hope.

'I'm saying that I'd be willing to hear what he has to say… I'll go in there with an open mind. I'm not making any promises, but I'm prepared to discuss it. I still think it's way too soon to go down that road.'

Her throat closed over with emotion. 'You'd do that for me?'

'It's only an appointment, Lara. Don't get excited…' he warned.

Eyes shining, she shook her head and flew at him, releasing a whoop as he whirled her around. 'When do we go?'

Their appointment with the specialist was arranged for the second month after they arrived in New York. Raoul arrived back early as arranged, only to find Lara sitting in exactly the same place she had been that morning when he'd left. She was still wearing her nightdress.

'What's happened?'

He dropped down on his knees beside the chair and took hold of her icy hands.

'I had a phone call from Lily.' She took a gulping swallow. 'It's Emmy—she's ill, in hospital.'

'Is it serious?'

She nodded. 'Very serious.' Her face crumpled. 'She might die…she's been ill awhile and Lily didn't even tell me.' It had brought home to her just how much her relationship with her twin had disintegrated.

'Oh, *cara*.' He pulled her into his arms. Lara pressed her face into his shoulder and sobbed.

'We'll fly out tomorrow. What about medical help? Tell her we will pay any—'

Lara lifted her tear-stained face and shook her head. 'I don't think she wants me there. If I were her I wouldn't want me there. And anyway, she doesn't need our help. Ben is loaded.'

'Who is Ben?'

'Ben Warrender. Emily Rose's father. I still can't believe it. We've known him for ever—his family own the estate…she didn't tell me. She sounded so…she must be going through hell!'

So, it seemed to him, was Lara.

'Have you cancelled the appointment?'

Lara looked at him blankly.

'The appointment with Dr Carlyle?'

'I forgot…will you ring them?'

'Of course I will,' he said, sliding his phone out and moving away to stand before the big glass window with its stunning view of Manhattan and the Hudson.

Lara sat there trying to pull herself together.

'Sorted, we can reschedule.'

'Thanks.' She dragged her hands through her hair before pressing them to her face. 'My brain isn't working. I just feel so helpless! I can't imagine how she is feeling and if she loses Emmy…'

'You *can* imagine,' he said softly. 'You lost a baby, Lara.'

Her fluttering glance flew to his face. 'It's not the same.'

Raoul, who did not think this the moment to discuss semantics, shrugged. 'You look terrible.' His compassionate gaze moved over her face. He held out his hand. 'Come on, you need some sleep. You're exhausted.'

After a moment she took his hand and allowed him to lead her to the bedroom, but each step felt like an effort.

She looked at the bed but didn't move. 'Will you make love to me, Raoul?' She asked it without looking at him. 'God knows, I could do with a bit of sympathy sex.' And she wasn't too proud to beg, but then she never was with Raoul.

Her love for him suddenly welled up inside her like a solid wall of emotion, and the intensity of it brought tears to her eyes. He didn't want her love, the only thing he wanted from her was a child and she couldn't even give him that.

She heard the sound of his rasped exclamation and turned her head. As she did so his mouth found hers; the kiss was deep, filled with passion and yet incredibly tender.

He laid her on the bed and without a word peeled away her nightclothes before taking off his own clothes and joining her in the bed.

She felt his whisper-light kiss on her face, against her closed eyelids. She kept her eyes closed as he pulled her to him, giving herself over completely to the pleasure of having his hands on her, his mouth on her. Raoul always knew where to touch her, how to touch her.

And when her body was ready, when the heat inside her built until only one thing could cool it, he slid into her, moving with deep strokes, letting them both enjoy being one. The combination of tenderness and passion brought tears of joy to her eyes as they shared the moment of ultimate bliss, their fevered cries blending into one.

As she felt him curl up against her back she reached behind her and caught his hand, curling it around her breast. She fell asleep with his hand on her heart and felt safe and loved, even though deep down she knew it was an illusion.

Finally, Lara got a tearful call from her sister. But the tears were good ones—Emmy was going to be all right. She rang Raoul immediately, wanting to share the good news, so it was frustrating when he didn't pick up.

She decided on impulse to cook him a special meal to celebrate. She had started to get to know some of the local stores and the novelty value of shopping in a new city had not worn off.

She got a bit carried away and bought way too much food. The bags tucked under her arms were bulging and heavy and there were still another few blocks to go before she reached the apartment building. About to admit defeat and hail a cab, she realised she was standing outside a coffee shop and realised why the name looked so familiar. A guide book she had bought had said that a coffee and Danish there while watching the world go by were an essential New York experience.

Seated at a table in the window, Lara savoured her Danish and her coffee. She wasn't convinced by it—the coffee tasted a bit funny—but she was definitely enjoying watching the world go by.

She was taking another bite of her Danish when she saw them. The pastry fell from her fingers.

Across the road on the steps of a hotel, her husband was kissing a dark-haired woman.

Lara felt as if someone had just thrust an icy

hand into her chest. The merciless fingers were squeezing her heart until it felt as though it would burst.

Was this how her mum had felt?

But I'm not my mum!

I won't *be her, I'm* not *going to run away and pretend I didn't see.* Shoulders squared, she got to her feet, the smooth lines of her face set with resolve. She'd had enough pretending.

'You forgot your groceries! Your bill!'

'Keep the groceries...' She pulled a bundle of notes from her purse and pushed them at the waiter. 'Keep the change!'

The lights changed and she ran; she was panting by the time she reached the other side of the street. Then, weaving her way through the scrum of people, she almost collided with the woman who was no longer in Raoul's arms but only a couple of feet away.

Lara registered several facts. The woman was Naomi and Raoul looked furious.

'Lara!'

She held up her hand. 'Later.' Turning her back on him, she faced the other woman. 'Look, I have no idea what your problem is, and frankly I don't want to. Just get the hell out of my life and leave my husband alone!'

A strangled squeaking noise left the woman's throat.

'Never make a redhead mad.'

Swallowing, Lara turned slowly back to Raoul. 'Never kiss women who are not your wife in public.'

His smile died. 'I was not doing the kissing, *cara*, she's deranged...' Eyes hard, he turned to Naomi. 'I am sorry your husband is divorcing you, but *we* do not have a relationship, *we* have never had a relationship, and I am not in love with you.'

'Believe him, Naomi, I do.' Whatever came between them, it would not be Naomi!

She barely registered the other woman's leaving as she took a step towards Raoul. 'And I *was* angry and hurt and...pretty much the way any woman who saw the man she loved kissing another woman would feel.'

She saw him stiffen.

'Lara—'

She ignored the warning in his voice. 'You don't want to hear this, I know, but, you see, I have to say it anyway. I'm sick of pretending,

Raoul. I love you, and I can't help it, and if you can't love me…' She bit her lips and shook her head. 'Well, I'd prefer to know—'

Looking at the appeal in the luminous eyes lifted to his, Raoul *wanted* to say he loved her, but the years of hardening his heart from the emotion, the knowledge of how it could destroy a man when it went wrong, stopped the words coming.

The seconds ticked by, and the fast thud of her heart slowed as her hope died, as Raoul stood there, silent, the muscles in his jaw flexing. A light drizzle had started, which was plastering his dark hair to his head.

She could wait for ever and he still wasn't going to say what she wanted to hear. Well, at least now she knew.

'It's fine,' she said, dying a little inside.

He squeezed his eyes closed to shut out the sight of her slender back as she walked away, fighting the irrational urge to follow her. It couldn't work, he reminded himself. He was the man he was, and incapable of returning what she had offered him.

And unworthy!

Why…*why* did she have to say it…?

* * *

Lara unlocked the door of the apartment and ran straight into the bathroom where she threw up violently.

After rinsing her mouth, she walked into the bedroom and, with a heart as empty as her stomach, she packed her belongings.

The note was short and to the point.

I'm going home. Please don't try and contact me. A baby deserves two parents who love one another.

There were no airport delays or incidents and her London-bound flight took off on time.

The hotel she booked into in the city was nondescript but it had everything she needed. Lara likened the instinct to a wounded dog crawling into a corner to lick its wounds—the trouble was a dog had better sense than to open and reopen the wound.

The concept of healing seemed a long way off. The numbness came and went in waves, and the rest of the time she was either murderously furious or depressingly self-pitying.

It wasn't until the third day that she realised

that nausea and vomiting were not just the symptoms of misery and heartache.

She couldn't be! Life could not be that cruel. She spent the rest of the day in the small box-like room telling herself it couldn't possibly be true.

She finally fell asleep around three a.m., wearing the red dress she'd had on when they first met—despair had made her masochistic, like an addiction that slowly killed you from the inside.

She had no idea what had made her pack it, or why she had even brought it to New York in the first place. Probably the same stupid, sentimental reason that had made her try it on the previous night.

She woke late feeling utterly wretched and no longer able to bury her head in the sand. She had to know.

The only thing she paused for on her way to the door was a painkiller, and then realised as she swallowed it that she'd accidentally taken one of the antihistamines that she used for hay fever.

Ah, well, the chemist would have something for her headache—as well as for the *other thing*.

She was halfway down the high street when she realised she was still wearing the dress she had slept in. Such was the sense of urgency that gripped her she didn't even consider going back to change.

The chemist had a ladies' room, and, rather than suffer another moment of the agony of not knowing, she used it. Then she went out, bought another testing kit, and went back in.

The result was the same.

She began to walk back to the hotel in a daze, experiencing a bitter sense of déjà vu when she missed her turning and found herself lost.

Pull yourself together, Lara! She rubbed a hand over her face, and realised the extra antihistamine was kicking in. Then, as if that weren't enough, her path was blocked by a loud and boisterous wedding party emerging from a register office.

There was the sound of popping corks as the happy couple emerged. At least her dress blended in with the other guests. Head down, she was trying to ease her way through the group when a guest carrying an open bottle of champagne in one hand and two glasses in the other backed into her.

Lara cried out as he trod down on her foot.

He swung around, accidentally depositing half the bottle of fizz down her dress. He stood there, an appalled look on his face. 'So sorry, I'm so sorry. Here.' He poured some of the remaining fizz into one of the glasses he held and pushed it at her.

'Have some, please, no hard feelings.'

It was easier and quicker to take a couple of small sips and 'accidentally' spill the rest rather than reject the misplaced token of generosity and apology. Lara had taken a few steps before she realised her mistake. She had barely swallowed a mouthful but with the antihistamines already in her system…she *had* to get back and sleep this off.

During the next five minutes the sense of urgency lessened. She was actually feeling quite mellow and then she saw—it seemed like fate—the man who had fathered her twin's child.

He was standing at a hotel entrance but he wasn't kissing anyone.

He'd been there for Lily, and for Emmy, and she had to thank him.

She had a memory of the look of horror on his face as she staggered over to him, but after that it was pretty much a blank. As Lily said when she sat with her before she cried herself to sleep, it was probably better that way.

CHAPTER FOURTEEN

THE SIGHT OF her sister the next morning made Lara feel even more of a disaster. Lily looked like the poster child for health and contentment. She was actually singing to herself; she was glowing.

'You never could hold a tune.'

Lily put down the apple she was peeling and came across to her sister. She put her hands on Lara's shoulders and looked into her face.

'There's flour on your nose. Have you gone all domestic?'

'Not really, I just had an urge to bake. It's very fashionable—hadn't you heard?'

'I'm sorry.' Lara looked around the room. 'Is he…?'

Lily shook her head. 'Ben thought he'd give us some time to catch up. He's taken Emmy to the park.'

Lara arched a satiric brow. 'You mean he's running scared of his lush of a sister-in-law. I only had a sip, you know…really. It just reacted with my hay-fever meds.'

'I explained that to him. He'll fetch your things over from the hotel. I can't believe that you've been here for two days and you didn't—'

'I needed time to think. And I was too ashamed,' Lara admitted. 'I wasn't even sure you'd want to see me. I was jealous.'

Lily nodded. 'I kind of worked that bit out… If I'd known about the baby…you are an idiot, you know that, don't you? I binned the dress. I hope that's all right…?'

Her life was binned, so why not?

'Half a bottle went down the front. I only had a sip. I promise, it was the allergy meds.'

'I know.'

'I don't know why I kept the dress,' Lara lied, then immediately confided, 'It was what I was wearing the first time I saw Raoul. I was feeling very sorry for myself and kind of masochistic.' She gave a gulping sob. 'I told him I loved him.'

'Some might say that it was about time.'

'I just couldn't keep it in any longer. I couldn't pretend…he never pretended to love me but deep down I thought…hoped that he'd follow me. But he didn't.'

'Does he know?'

Lara lifted her head from her twin's shoulder. 'Know?'

'That you're pregnant.' She saw her sister's expression and shook her head, smiling. 'No, I'm not psychic and you're not showing. You told me last night. You told me a lot of things.'

Lara's eyes fell. 'No, he doesn't,' she murmured.

'From what you've said I'm guessing he'd come running if he knew.'

Lara nodded. 'Yes, he would. That's what makes it so hard... I... I... Thanks.' She gave a watery smile, accepting the wad of tissues Lily pressed into her hand, and she pulled out a stool at the breakfast bar. 'I was tempted. I thought I could settle but I want more, Lily.'

'You deserve more. Are you really so sure that he doesn't love you? I mean, whenever I've seen him he can't take his eyes off you.'

'It's a part he's playing, a part we both were, but for me it became real.' She stopped and gave a wild little laugh. 'No, I'm still lying. That's not true—it was love at first sight for me... I know, how crazy is that?'

Her twin didn't join in her laughter. 'I don't think it's crazy at all.'

'But then you always were the romantic…not me.' She ran her tongue across her dry lips and shook her head, her voice dropping to a grief-laden whisper as she admitted, 'If I hadn't been pregnant when his grandfather died the marriage would have ended then—that was the plan.'

'Well, if a baby was never part of the plan you both seem to have gone to a lot of trouble to make it happen,' Lily observed.

'I was devastated. I hadn't known how much I wanted it.' She swallowed down hard. 'He just felt sorry for me and there was the heir thing, carrying on his name.'

'I wish you'd told me.'

Lara gave a watery smile. 'How could I? You were pregnant and—I wanted to be happy for you, I *was* happy for you, but I was also jealous,' she admitted with a shamed sniff.

'If you don't mind me saying, Lara, your hus-band has never struck me as the sort of man who makes life-changing decisions because of pity.'

Lara blinked. 'No,' she conceded. 'But…he has a strong sense of duty, family. He can be very

protective. You know, I used to believe that who-
ever I fell in love with would naturally love me
back, because…because that's just the way it's
supposed to be. But perhaps this is some of sort
of punishment for being so conceited, because
I've tried and I've tried and—' She squeezed
her eyes closed as the anguished words emerged
from her aching throat. 'But I can't make him
love me.' Head bent, she closed her eyes. 'And I
can't live without being loved.'

'Neither can I, Lara.'

She hugged her twin and added huskily, 'I'm
glad that you have Ben, you sneaky old thing. If
anyone deserves to be happy after all you've been
through it's you.' She gave a sudden choking sob
and wailed, 'Raoul deserves to be happy too.'

'You know you have to tell him about the baby.'

'Do you think I don't know that?'

He had let her walk away. As he turned and
walked in the opposite direction he could still
hear her saying it: *I love you.*

People took one look at his stony face and took
hasty detours around the tall man as Raoul strode
out blindly, feeding his anger as the emotions

inside him built. She knew the rules, she was the one who had broken them, this *could* have worked…it *was* working.

Then his anger vanished and he clenched his jaw against the hit of guilt as he remembered the hope shining in her eyes, and how it had died and vanished as she'd waited for him to respond.

It had been a brave thing to do, a *Lara* thing. She'd had hope and he'd crushed it. Angry with her for saying it, but tortured by the thought of her hurting, he walked on, his black thoughts a swirl of self-loathing, anger and resentment.

He'd let her walk away.

Why?

He waited for the accusatory stream of responses to come—*she* wasn't being fair, *she* was asking for something he couldn't give, he was doing her a favour because *she* deserved—but they didn't come.

He stopped dead.

They were lies.

The truth flayed him and he didn't avoid the pain, he deserved it!

Lara was brave, and he was a coward, a gutless wonder who'd been too scared to admit his own feelings even to himself. And why? Because he'd stopped trusting his own feelings, and his solution was to pretend he didn't have any.

And it hadn't been that hard until Lara had appeared. She had challenged his accepted way of thinking from day one; she'd awoken dormant emotions inside him and made them blaze up like an out-of-control fire.

Once love had almost destroyed him, it had simply never even entered his consciousness that love, *real* love, could also be a salvation.

Lara was his salvation and he'd let her walk away.

He felt power surge through him as he embraced the truth: Lara was the love of his life. He was going to fix things, he was going to lay his heart at her feet and beg her to take him back.

It had been a massive anticlimax when he'd got back to the apartment and she wasn't there...just that heartbreaking note.

Raoul hadn't slept since. He'd traced her to London and then Lara seemed to have vanished. He felt as though he'd aged ten years in the last three days. He was crazy with worry; he'd tried everything...everyone.

If she wasn't here, he thought as the taxi driver pulled up outside a house in a leafy road, he didn't know what he'd do.

'Is this it?'

'I hope so,' Raoul breathed, paying off the driver. 'I really hope so.' He'd finally tracked down her sister, who was at a new address, and if she didn't know where Lara was then he wasn't sure what his next move would be.

He rang the bell and the door opened immediately. Seeing another woman with his wife's face, after so many days without her, was a jolt.

'Is she here?'

She looked him up and down, her eyes narrowed and assessing before responding. 'She is— she's through that way. No!' She laid a hand flat on his chest to stop his impulsive progress. 'Listen, Lara is…she's kind of fragile right now and if you hurt her, so help me, Mr Di Vittorio, you'll be singing soprano. Message received?'

'Received, and, for the record, though I am very attached to my singing voice I would sooner lose it than hurt Lara.'

Lily smiled and stepped back to let him pass, yelling after him, 'Don't mess it up!'

* * *

'I have been looking for you.'

With a gasp Lara turned, jumping up off the stool she sat on. She pressed her hands against her chest, fighting down the urge to reach out and touch him.

Instead in a flat little voice she said, 'It's over.'

'Let me finish! I have been looking for you *all my life*, though I didn't realise it. I would not let myself believe it. Lucy…she left me feeling toxic, like I had nothing left to give another woman, and then when I found you I was too stupid and cowardly…yes!' he said, reacting to her little whimper of protest with a shake of his head. 'Too cowardly to face the truth. I loved you, Lara Gray, from the moment I saw you. You are my life and I am nothing without you. I am here to beg you to have me. We will live where you like—move here to England if that is what you want—have IVF, adopt, do whatever you want. It is true, I am a bastard…a stupid, selfish bastard…' he said in a voice that throbbed with the depth of his conviction.

Raoul had been taking slow deliberate steps towards her as he spoke, but he stopped now that his dark eyes fastened on her face.

Could it be true?

Unable any longer to hold it in, she said the words he had ached to hear again. 'I love you, Raoul. I love you so much, I couldn't keep it in any longer. I thought all you wanted from me was an heir, and I wanted so…so much to give you one because I thought you didn't want me—'

The rest of her confession was lost in his mouth. Raoul crushed her to him, drinking in the taste of her, his hands moulding her body to his.

He framed her face with his hands and looked down into her eyes. 'I can't believe I just stood there. I can't believe I thought it would be easier to be alone and lonely than risk my heart. When I think what I could have lost… When I came back and found you gone I— Never, *ever* do that to me again. If you knew the things I have been imagining…'

'It was awful,' she admitted. 'It tore me apart…' She took a deep breath. 'I've decided against the IVF.'

A shade of caution flickered into his dark eyes.

'I found out yesterday that I'm pregnant.'

Joy filled his face. 'Perfect!' He kissed her and added throatily, 'You are perfect, and you must not worry this time—'

She pressed a finger to his lips. 'I am not worried, not while I have you,' she said simply. Whatever life threw at her, with Raoul at her side they would come through, together.

Neither heard the noise as the front door swung open.

Lily stood there pulling on her coat, blocking the way of Ben, who wielded a pushchair containing a sleeping child.

'We have to go back out!' she whispered.

'Why?'

'Lara is in there—'

'Oh, God, is she drunk again?'

'No, you idiot, she's not drunk. She's in love!'

* * * * *

If you enjoyed this story,
check out these other great reads from
Kim Lawrence

HER NINE MONTH CONFESSION
THE SINS OF SEBASTIAN REY-DEFOE
ONE NIGHT WITH MORELLI
THE HEARTBREAKER PRINCE
A SECRET UNTIL NOW

Available now!

MILLS & BOON®
Large Print – August 2016

The Sicilian's Stolen Son
Lynne Graham

Seduced into Her Boss's Service
Cathy Williams

The Billionaire's Defiant Acquisition
Sharon Kendrick

One Night to Wedding Vows
Kim Lawrence

Engaged to Her Ravensdale Enemy
Melanie Milburne

A Diamond Deal with the Greek
Maya Blake

Inherited by Ferranti
Kate Hewitt

The Billionaire's Baby Swap
Rebecca Winters

The Wedding Planner's Big Day
Cara Colter

Holiday with the Best Man
Kate Hardy

Tempted by Her Tycoon Boss
Jennie Adams

0716 Rom LP

MILLS & BOON®
Large Print – September 2016

Morelli's Mistress
Anne Mather

A Tycoon to Be Reckoned With
Julia James

Billionaire Without a Past
Carol Marinelli

The Shock Cassano Baby
Andie Brock

The Most Scandalous Ravensdale
Melanie Milburne

The Sheikh's Last Mistress
Rachael Thomas

Claiming the Royal Innocent
Jennifer Hayward

The Billionaire Who Saw Her Beauty
Rebecca Winters

In the Boss's Castle
Jessica Gilmore

One Week with the French Tycoon
Christy McKellen

Rafael's Contract Bride
Nina Milne

0816 Rom LP

MILLS & BOON®

Why shop at millsandboon.co.uk?

Each year, thousands of romance readers find their perfect read at millsandboon.co.uk. That's because we're passionate about bringing you the very best romantic fiction. Here are some of the advantages of shopping at www.millsandboon.co.uk:

* **Get new books first**—you'll be able to buy your favourite books one month before they hit the shops

* **Get exclusive discounts**—you'll also be able to buy our specially created monthly collections, with up to 50% off the RRP

* **Find your favourite authors**—latest news, interviews and new releases for all your favourite authors and series on our website, plus ideas for what to try next

* **Join in**—once you've bought your favourite books, don't forget to register with us to rate, review and join in the discussions

Visit **www.millsandboon.co.uk**
for all this and more today!